# SWEET OLD WORLD

## - New & Selected Stories -

BRIAN LEYDEN

ISBN-13: 978-1508415602
ISBN-10: 1508415609

Dedicated to Carmel

# CONTENTS

# THE LAST MINING VILLAGE

THEY SAID THE COALMINES would not last much longer. And it seemed, with every passing week, another one of the old characters had gone to that dauby graveyard on the hill.

Picture a valley by a lake below an iron and rusty-red mountain. Add a pub, a parish hall, two grocers' shops, scattered housing, a bridge, a river and a loose knot of coal-and-oil-black roads.

On Easter Sunday morning outside an immaculate church, bright as the pearly gates, gleaming lines of family cars grace the car park below the church and graveyard. A church bell tolls, calling the respectable, responsible citizens of the valley to mass. A late-comer trips up the steps, creaks and bangs the door, turns all heads, and slips, shamefaced, into a seat at the back. Then the hushed and prosperous Sunday morning stillness.

Dark figures shuffle in the church porch. They crouch and whisper over the prayers, sermon, coughs and bells of the mass going on inside. They talk about coal mines, cattle and current affairs.

"I hear the Germans bought a farm over on the far mountain."

"You don't buy a farm over there, you buy an address."

The sun breaks through the stained-glass windows above the altar and scatters like confetti across the aisle. It is after half-past eleven. The men outside listen for sounds of the crowd stirring.

"Go forth in peace."

"Amen."

And the race is on. The shopkeeper's assistant is out the door like a shot off a shovel. A quick blessing and they pour out the church

1

door like dark treacle running down the steps. Engines throb to life, misty exhausts fume in the car park. Men and women and children bolt down the road with unbuttoned best coats. The clicking and clacking of high heels kicking up the gravel and dry leaves under a chestnut tree as old as the valley. It is neck and neck all the way to the paper-seller's hut.

The finishing post is an always-open-on-Sundays shop where the crowd will always be there before you. Women with Sunday dinners on their minds, lined six-deep at the counter. Calling for freshly roasted chickens, frozen peas, carrots, cauliflower and ice-cream, litres of lemonade, sweet cakes and something for the supper. And treats for scrubbed children on their Sunday best behaviour.

Outside, patient men in long coats and white, open-neck shirts shuffle around the pub door, like the mourners of Lazarus waiting for the miraculous opening of the tomb. What do they care about the black-coat-and-hat brigade of pious tooth-suckers, tut-tutting as they pass, swallowing Eucharist and gossip between lips as severe as a Good Friday collation.

With righteous heads held high they aim their sharp, viper tongues at a certain big redheaded, loud-laughing, pint-loving lout sporting an outlawed Easter lily, sideburns, cowboy boots and baggy trousers from a mart-day stall.

"He didn't get that head drinking spring water."

The easy Sunday babble of the river follows the good people walking home from mass. In the pub the Sunday drinkers discuss work, jobs, money and the future. Over the rim of the frosted glass in the bar-room window, heaps of wet coal glitter on the dark hill overlooking the pub.

*"There's a race of men that don't fit in*
*They'd break the heart of kith and kin*
*They'd break the heart of a stone*
*Break the heart of a stone."*

The big man whispers into his drink. But nobody is listening.

Establish your credentials here with a pint. And sitting at the bar, overhear a yarn about Francie the barber, who lived by the church and shaved the priest for beer-money.

"Do you remember the morning Francie got the shakes and he drew blood with the old cut-throat razor? And the priest said:

"That's the drink for you, Francie."

2

"I know, Father, it leaves the skin very tender."

The ganger Gaffney adds to the legend, and he tells the company about the time the same priest was walking back to his house after saying mass when he met Francie, staggering past the chapel, on his way home from the pub.

"I'm warning you now, Francie, you're on the very brink of hell.'

"Didn't they build it very close to the church, Father?"

Outside, the shrill yelps of children. Out of nowhere the travelling fair has arrived. Each year it comes mysteriously, like the first snow. Brightly painted and always harbouring some dark secret behind the painted shutters. And always a mad dog chained at the back of the slumbering caravans. The children haggle for silver from their parents and mount the rides with rough glee. Screams of delight pierce the brittle air. All is harmless now in the hard light of day. It will only develop its special, sinister magic when darkness falls. When the fairground music echoes the length of the valley and the whir and clatter of the rides mingle with boisterous shouts of young and old. When the blue dusk falls like magic powder on the eternal fairground and restores to life swing-boats, rifle-ranges, bumper-cars, and a childlike sense of wonder.

Once upon a time hard men walked the valley. Those were the days of gang fights, Paisley shirts and broad ties, purple suits with matching waistcoats, bell-bottom trousers and platform shoes. After a week of hacking deep in the belly of the mountain the weekends were given over to drinking and fighting. To days of longstanding rivalry between the country dance-halls that served nothing stronger than minerals and bags of cheese-and-onion crisps.

Long lines of Honda fifties - twenty-five or more - circled the village in clouds of summer dust, and then trailed off to a neighbouring parish. Looking for trouble and usually finding it: fist-fights and broken furniture, torn jackets, blood on white shirt-fronts. Split lips, bleeding noses.

Or drinking all day before a feed of burgers and white soup at the chipper, and then on to the Mayflower ballroom. To hear Joe Dolan or Margo or Big Tom.

The crowded cloakrooms, the empty dance-floors. Girls dancing together, steps rehearsed at home or in school corridors; long lines of girls sitting with their backs to the wall.

And the crush: that body of youths milling close to the sweaty walls, tightly packed, like prisoners chained to the pillar, going round and round asking every girl in the line for a dance.

"Will you come for a slither on the boards?"

"Will you lean up against me for this one?"

"Would you ever hold me pint, I'm bursting for a...."

"No... No.... No...."

Though, of course, there was always one big-hearted girl like that last turkey on the supermarket shelf; everybody had a squeeze but nobody took her home.

In the slippery, wet-floored, reeking toilets the young men slick back their hair before returning to the crush to try their luck or, perhaps, their looks again. And standing at the urinal you hear a low, serious conversation. Two boys with slurred voices face one another.

In the wink of an eye one goes down. Blink and you miss that smart smack to the jaw, that gush of blood from a burst lip, that sudden buckling at the knees before he slumps to the floor.

One man lies stretched and another man with bruised knuckles and dead eyes, breathing beer and onions, leans up against you and says:

"He was asking for that."

And you'd be a fool to disagree.

There was always more action at the door, where the trouble with the bouncers started. Big men, like sides of meat with bow-ties on, who always seemed to be looking for a fight. And you could look on at the minor scuffles among the colliers and doormen and recall one mad, full-moon night when the ballroom came under siege.

Stones were thrown through windows and the bouncers kneeled under the broken panes like cowboys cornered in a western saloon. Then somebody tossed a motorbike through the window. A red and white Honda fifty crash-landed on the dance-floor and the bouncers fled for home. Chased all the way to the county border by youths yelling abuse out the windows of Ford cars.

Cars were made for cowboys then. The bog-standard old Ford Escort, with extra-heavy springs in the back. And the king of cars, the mark two Cortina E in chrome and black, with furry dice, simulated leopard-skin seat covers, a cassette player warbling country music and a cardboard air-freshener with a naked girl hanging from the rear-view mirror. Back seat romances, reclining front seats and smoochy music. How many couples stepped into marriage through

4

the passenger doors of those second-hand cars?

After every summer there were casualties. Hurried marriages before it showed. And on and on it goes: long after the furtive encounters at the backs of dance-halls, long after the passing of the ballroom days the romance, the bouncing springs, the steamed-up windows remain. In hotel carparks where the discos are the new kings crowned with coloured spotlights. A new generation is born, but habits remain the same. Second-hand cars, dances, fights and childhood codes of honour.

*"Eggs and rashers for the Arigna smashers,*
*Hay and oats for the Drumshanbo goats."*

And then, shortly after that first shave with his father's razor, he drops his school bag for a pit helmet, and the promise of freedom bought with a working man's wage.

The pit lorry passes the school bus and a pale-faced student looks over at black, grimy-faced pals: tired but suddenly grown-up men in tattered working clothes, working off a bellyful of last night's porter.

"What does your father do?"

"He works in the power-station."

"Shovelling light into dark corners."

Memories of innocence before hard labour. Before adult rites of passage in the dark mines and bars. And a question for a bystander:

"You never worked in the pits yourself?"

"I'll be long enough underground."

We have all gone our own ways now. But we remember common ground.

The national school was built three miles away from the village centre; as the pitmen headed to work the scholars set out for school. Walking the long road to a day in school whose only reward was the journey home. A journey past hay-barns and orchards. Orchards with sour green crab-apples that tasted like nectar, protected by a notice saying "Trespassers Will Be Prosecuted". And still you dared, and you had to reach through the mossy branches for the reddest, sweetest apple that was, always, at the top of the tree.

On the way home "Poodle" Dean drank water from the puddles and ate earthworms for a dare. And everybody stamped on the hosts of flying ants, because you never forgave them for their stings, years ago, when you sat on their nests by accident in short trousers, and found your pants full of pismires.

But it is all changing so fast. New schools and new open-cast mines. In the old days they sank mine-shafts here. Tunnelled their way to the seams of coal. The men marched underground, a hundred or more working in one mine. Foreheads lit by pale flames from brassy, bubbling carbide-and-water lamps hanging on their helmets. Swallowed up each morning by the open mouth of the pit. Only a glimmering thread of lights leading in to their private, subterranean world. And a long steel cable fishing out lines of hutches. Rattling out on narrow rails, and loaded with shiny, black lumps of coal.

The lorries, painted red then, rumbled down the valley and rattled back empty from the habitually smoking power-station with its tall chimney like a balanced cigarette on Lough Allen's shore. Above the noise of conveyor belts, pumps and air compressors came the screech of the sawmill, where pillars and props - that would soon be creaking and bending under the dripping wet weight of the mountain - were cut. But no more.

The old mines are closing. Slowly turning to places of ghosts and memories. The wealth of coal exhausted. The old shafts have been sealed up and regiments of conifers press in on these abandoned places. Graveyards marked with mechanical headstones. It would take a child or an artist to find beauty now in places so full of rain, rust and ruin. Among the tangled remains of broken hutch-wheels. Among fallen-down sheds and shattered windows and broken rails. Among rusty, serpent-coils of steel rope and bent pipes scattered to the wind like drinking straws. Among the ghost voices of long dead men and their fiercely guarded ways.

The Sunday drinkers are having one for the road; the yarns are all told, the painted shutters are going up on the fairground booths. Dinners and papers, wives and children, the Sunday football game and the afternoon snooze are waiting amongst the bungalows. And far from schoolhouses and dance-halls, far from fairgrounds and bars, far from scandals and prayers, far from pits and power-station, the road takes me away from a valley by a lake below a mountain.

# LAST REMAINS

MRS MCDAID ALWAYS SAT IN the kitchen in an armchair, smoked dark brown by the open fire. Reading religious magazines with names like *The Sacred Heart* and *The African Mission*, *The Far East* and *The Messenger*. She was my granny, and people said she was a very pious woman. I was afraid of her.

We lived only a short distance down the road from my grandparents then. And each evening I had to fetch a sweet-can full of hot, frothy milk from the farm. I always avoided the kitchen window, going down the cobbled back-yard directly to the barn where Henry Joe McDaid did the milking.

If I came early I would help Henry Joe by driving in the cattle. He would wait in the yard, searching the clouds at the butt of the hill for tomorrow's weather. With savage shouts I would bluster and threaten the rheumatic cattle: "come-up-out-of-that," who came trudging and creaking through the rushes at their own pace, spattering my bare legs with cow-clung.

When the cattle were tied at their stakes I stood in the doorway teasing flakes of whitewash from the stone walls. The barn was big, warm and thatched with generations of cobwebs woven through the rafters. I listened to the splish-splash regular rhythm, as his two strong hands drew white strokes from the swollen udders into a galvanised iron bucket. When he finished he dipped his finger into the froth on the milk and drew a cross on the cow's flank as a blessing with the cow chewing away like the old woman of the house.

Granny McDaid came out to strain the milk through a square of muslin, measuring out my three pints with great exactness. She hobbled about on arthritic legs and a bad hip, supported by an evil-looking blackthorn walking stick.

"Off with you now, before it gets dark," she would gesture with her stick. "Before the pookey man gets you."

Thursday was churning day. Mrs McDaid stood over the wooden butter churn in the flagstone-floored outhouse Henry Joe called the 'Dairy'. Henry Joe and myself fetched and carried for her. Running with kettles of scalding water, or carrying between us the big black and red earthenware crocks, with smooth lids of clotted cream.

Mrs McDaid operated the dash, her mottled hands gripping the long handle going through the lid of the barrel-shaped churn. Henry Joe had made that dash at his bench in the cart-shed where he kept his oilstones, handsaws, spokeshave, spirit level, chisels and blades in bright order, and cut the magic pattern through which the old woman pumped the milk into butter.

"Bad cess to it, it doesn't make proper butter," she would up-cast to him.

Then she called for more hot water, with her red-rimmed eyes on the thermometer in its wooden jacket, or a bucket of cold water from the well had to be spilt on the flagstone floor to regulate the surrounding temperature. Finally, I ran for cups to taste the buttermilk, rags to wipe the lid, salt and strainer. We gazed into the pungent depths of the churn and looked down on the pale clots of butter floating on the steaming milk or stuck to the grain in the sides of the wooden churn.

I was reared on the taste of Blue Band margarine and I hated the strong flavour of that colourless and salty country butter which the old woman patted into ovals with her wrinkly hands.

Though the butter tasted disgusting to me, and though I was always getting things wrong or being told to get out from under the old woman's feet, I never missed churning day. For each time the lid of the churn was raised that purest sense of wonder struck as the miracle of the making of the butter was revealed.

Every Friday evening I brought the milk money to Mrs McDaid. I dreaded the evenings I didn't have the exact change. Then I would have to help the old woman up the stairs to her bedroom. A room which was always locked. She kept the key on the end of a shoe-lace which was pinned somewhere inside the many folds and layers of her cardigans and skirts.

I would stand by the door as the lock clicked and she heaved herself up the last step into the sinister bedroom. After a long wait I sometimes worked up the courage to steal a glimpse of the room. There was a heavy wooden crucifix nailed up on the wall over her candlewick bedspread, ringed by pictures and prints of jaundice-yellow and gloomy apostles. More saints and wounded martyrs watched over a big wardrobe stuffed with coats and dresses from Yankee parcels. There was a dressing table smothered in bottles and holy water vessels, medications, tablets, ointments and rubs. The room smelt of camphor and mothballs, holy candles, medicine and her.

I waited as she rustled and poked through the top drawer of her dressing table, sifting big, old-money paper notes; fire-brick red ten-shilling notes, green pounds with the picture of the woman with the harp on the front, and huge notes with river gods on the back, in rainbow shades of mauve and blue.

My eyes fell to the floor again when she came hobbling out with the change. Unlike Henry Joe she never offered me a couple of age-blackened halfpennies, or a big brown penny the full size of my fist for an expedition to the shop for bull's-eyes, penny biscuits or a lucky bag.

With the proper change in an envelope in my pocket, safely sealed and addressed to my mother, I had to link her down the stairs again. The old woman always came down steps and stairs backways. Clinging to the banisters on one side and me on the other. I suffered her weight and her cold touch and the smell of Vick's ointment and waited with her each time she told me she had to stop to "rift gas".

On Sunday mornings Granny McDaid arranged for a hackney man to bring everybody to first mass. Escorted by Henry Joe on one side and my father on the other, wearing her pearl-brooched and best black coat with the fur collar, Yankee bonnet and veil, she led the procession of neighbours up the length of the church and took her proper place in the front seat with the padded kneeling board nearest the altar.

I would sit fidgeting by her side, while Mrs McDaid mouthed her prayers, always a full blessing ahead of the priest. Having suffered the compulsory fast before communion, the smell of rashers on the pan and Denny's pork sausages dipped in a soft fried egg invaded my nostrils, in anticipation of the soon to be had ritual fry for Sunday breakfast in our warm kitchen at home. The mass seemed to last an eternity and afterwards we had to wait for Mrs McDaid to finish her private chat with the priest and the darling altar boys.

Canon Daly, a man feared by every school-going or mitching child in the half-parish, came to visit Mrs McDaid's house on the first Friday of every month. Confessions were heard and rumours exchanged. From these talks with both parish priest and canon, together with the gossip gathered every Saturday on her visits to the medical dispensary, she knew that the entire village was a hotbed of heedless spending and ungodly appetites

Every first Friday after the Canon left I would sit and listen to her giving out about "that trollop" who stood behind the village bar. And then she sucked her teeth over the sinful sums of money taken in across the glass-bottom-ringed counter from those shameless slaves to Arthur Guinness.

When I got home my mother would send me to the pub to ask Henry Joe and my father if they were ready to come home. A mission which always involved a wait on a high padded seat in the smoky front bar, rewarded with a mineral and a bag of crisps as another round of pints mysteriously appeared.

On Friday mornings Henry Joe always sat in the square of light close to the kitchen window, his elbows resting on the oilcloth, while Mrs McDaid sat in her chair by the fire calling out her wants: Andrews liver salts, baking soda, Fry's cocoa, Birds's custard, Fiery Jack's liniment, sugar - in case of another shortage - and a half-quarter of tobacco, which was Henry Joe's reward.

Then she would stop to make up the prices in her head, her idea being that the total bill for the shopping should leave Henry Joe without the price of a drink. At the same time the bill should not be too great. Then the balance would have to be taken out of her own pension money.

Henry Joe's only defence was to keep the bit of paper on which the list was written very small. He quartered an already tiny sheet of paper taken from an airmail writing pad, using his oiled and surgically sharp pocket-knife. Then he fished out the shiny metal case where he kept his spectacles and a stubby blue pencil. After teasing the wire frames around his ears he scraped a needle fine point on the pencil to copy each item down in his meticulous, miniscule handwriting.

Granny McDaid took a long time before calling out each article as she added up the prices under her breath. When she finally lapsed into silence Henry Joe folded up his square of paper, put away the end of pencil, and tucked the list neatly in under his glasses in the silver case, which he deposited in the inside pocket of his second-best jacket, the one with the leatherette patches on the elbows. Mrs McDaid, having decided that the total bill was still less than Henry Joe's entire pension money, then called out another item.

"Can't you leave it at that woman? There's no room on the list."

"Well, get another bit of paper, you dunder-head."

Henry Joe might have put away the spectacle-case five or six times and have as many separate scraps of paper with additions to the original list before Granny fetched their pension books from the dressing table upstairs, and added her official signature like a woman signing the Proclamation. Despite which she always got her sums wrong and Henry Joe could be found every Friday evening in the pub enjoying a drink with the coal miners at the end of their shift.

By the time my mother would have given the order to fetch Henry Joe and my father home from the public house a crowd would have gathered around old Henry Joe McDaid. The company was lively because Henry Joe always had a puzzle, a riddle or a mathematics problem. He had a fresh problem every week, and for these his audience divided into two camps. One camp gave him a fair hearing, pausing over their pints to puzzle out Henry Joe's new conundrum.

"There's more ways to kill a cat than choke him with butter," Henry Joe would announce, after every wrong answer. A pub regular in wellingtons, called Tom Packie, with a full company of barfly supporters, acted fool in the middle. After Tom Packie volunteered a particularly stupid answer Henry Joe would wheel around and inform him: "The hens in our yard have more brains."

On a second attempt he might add: "If you said that to our ass, he'd kick you."

But the good boys were only happy with the evening if they led old Henry Joe to dance on his hat with frustration. Then the woman from behind the bar settled the argument, spun the green-lit wireless dial to Athlone, and took Henry Joe out for an old-time waltz until it was time to go home.

Henry Joe always arrived back merry and red-faced, and in good appetite for his favourite boiled flat Dutch cabbage, bacon marbled with fat and soda-bread plastered with salty home-made butter that Mrs McDaid reluctantly served him, with her proper pension money and the groceries delivered earlier by the shop van, all present and in order. She was forced to take to her chair by the fire, severe but silent, and sip on her liver salts.

She had to wait for the next day to launch her attack. On Saturdays Henry Joe stretched himself out on the brown wooden settle-bed in the kitchen corner, his hat pulled down over his eyes, his head in his hands, and no man at death's door ever moaned louder or felt more sorry for himself.

Then, one stiff and grey winter Saturday, Mrs McDaid headed for the medical dispensary in a hired car, a trip she made, hail or ailing, every Saturday of the year. When the doctor had finished his examination, and had given her two kinds of tablets, he left, as usual, by the back door. Mrs McDaid returned to an empty waiting room, with no sign of the hackney man outside. Tom Packie and a neighbour found her stranded in the front porch.

"You can't stay there, Mrs McDaid. Come on with us. We'll link you as far as the pub. You can sit at the fire while we ring for another hackney man."

The roads were icy, the wind bitterly cold, and Mrs McDaid consented. The two men linked her to the public house.

"You'll have a hot one with us? A whiskey, Mrs McDaid, with hot water, a pinch of sugar and a few cloves. Sure, it'll take the chill out of your bones."

It was a bitterly cold day and she had been waiting a long time. She drank the hot whiskey down and Tom Packie went to the bar for another. Some people said she just took a bad turn, but most agreed afterwards it was the strong spirits combined with the tablets she had taken such a short time before that killed her.

"The Lord between us and all harm," said Tom Packie, catching her as she fell.

And for years to come, whenever Tom Packie got very drunk he would say: "She died in me arms, God rest her. Right in that very spot," pointing towards the seat under the window engraved with the legend, "Powers Whiskey".

I was on the front street, watching Henry Joe pull a length of string through a ball of pitch to make cobbler's thread, or wax-end as he called it, when the procession arrived from the village. They carried the body into the front parlour and then they brought down Henry Joe's settle-bed from the kitchen and left Mrs McDaid out on that until the room upstairs was ready. Two neighbouring women were sent for to wash and dress the corpse. Tom Packie carried water for them.

When Mrs McDaid was laid out properly in her own room, I crept in to see her. The women had fitted a shroud with a holy picture on the chest and combed back her hair which was surprisingly long. There was a Bible and a wedge of tissue under her chin to keep the mouth closed and a black rosary beads threaded through her fingers.

The curtains were drawn and the only light came from two blessed candles alongside the silver crucifix with the round base used for a station in the house. I had never seen a dead person before and could not grasp the depth of silence that surrounded the corpse, or the utter absence of all the things that had made Granny McDaid such a fearful old woman.

Now Mrs McDaid died in a crowded pub on a Saturday afternoon, and news of her passing spread fast and wide. A crowd of people soon gathered in the McDaid house, the number swelling fast with a constant stream of callers coming in ones and twos and hushed parties of four.

Mrs McDaid's two younger sisters met the people inside the door. Tom Packie was dispatched to the pub, taking me along with him for the spin. The first job was to buy drink for the wake. His order was generous, being funded from the rustling top-drawer of Mrs McDaid's dressing table. He loaded the boot and the well of the hackney man's old Ford with boxes of shopping, extra bread and rattling cases of booze until there was scarcely enough room for the driver and himself, with me sitting on the handbrake.

We visited the undertaker next to order the casket, phone the times of the removal and the funeral to the papers, and to arrange the marking out of the plot where the neighbouring men would dig the grave in turns.

The winding clock over the fireplace was put away when the corpse was brought into the house. The early winter evening fell with the McDaid sisters passing out pipe-tobacco and saucers filled with cigarettes, and every caller was met with a drink.

Big-bosomed women bedecked in black, with bottles of porter, naggins of whiskey, steaming teapots, ham sandwiches, home-made currant cake, blessed candles and bottle openers, milk jugs, sugar bowls, and trembling grips that were a danger to my mother's good china, were bossily in charge for the night.

By midnight there was broken glass on the kitchen floor where bottles had fallen over and the flagstones were slippery with treacle-black stout. A crowd of people lined the stairs where spilt beer ran from step to step. Men clutching whiskey bottles told the funniest and the oldest yarns of great characters long dead. Distant relatives appeared. Fighting neighbours shook hands. And Henry Joe was settled quietly in a corner. It was my job to look after him, but he didn't move or say a word the whole night.

"She'd never have approved of the drinking," said Tom Packie, throwing back a half-one with his little finger in the air, "but it's a grand wake all the same."

"I'm thinking we won't see the likes of it again in our time," said another pub stalwart. "God be with the old wakes, when there was music in the kitchen and matchmaking in the hall, and a cow turned out of the barn for a tumble in the warm spot."

"I won't stand for that kind of talk under this roof," said Tom Packie. "She was a decent woman, God rest her. One of the old sort."

"Lord have mercy," they said in unison.

It was long past my bedtime when the old women arranged for a rosary to be said over the corpse before the family moved in to keep their all-night vigil. I pushed my way up through the crowd on the stairs and went into the bedroom, where I kneeled next to the door as the old women called out their sorrowful mysteries.

When the rosary was said several of the late callers placed their hands lightly over the hands of the corpse before quitting the room. Tom Packie was standing behind me. He prodded me in the back.

"Touch the corpse," he said.

I was still stunned by her passing, and by the sight of that pale form lying there between the cold, white cotton sheets. As I crossed the room I was dimly aware that I was a witness to the passing of a hard-won, self-sufficient world. Witness to the passing of the last remains of brown wooden settle-beds and barrel butter churns, winding pocket watches and guessing at the weather from the front street, Yankee dresses and parcels, sixpenny bits and forms, old women ramblers and callers to the well for water, late night card-games and ghost stories told by the fire, with sworn sightings of will-o'-the-wisps and the wandering dead.

I reached out my hand, then took it back quickly. Her skin had the same cold wax feel as a church candle. Tom Packie nodded, and then ushered me out of the room. With his hand left on my shoulder he said: "You have to touch the corpse, or you'll dream about her tonight."

# CHRISTMAS PROMISE

THE DAY AFTER WE GET the Christmas holidays we take the bus to a crowded shopping town with my mother. Her lists made out, the money carefully rolled in a big black purse with a brass clip, she walks my younger brother and me to the crossroads in our nylon anoraks. There is an excited hurry in our step as we trot the country mile to the main road. My brother swings his arms to keep up the pace while my mother watches the time on a small gold wrist-watch. We get there a few minutes early, our foreheads hot and our scalps tingling.

"It's not gone yet."

"That's if it's coming at all."

Breakdowns and abandoned journeys are frequent and we worry until we sight the sun-flash of the driver's big windshield, the red and white coachwork lurching towards us, taking up most of the road and pulling up tight against the ditch as we come around the front to the open door. The driver searches a school exercise book with the fares written in blue biro while my mother stands with the right money already in her fist.

Down the middle aisle we make our way, minding our paper tickets. A small man with his hands in his lap smiles at us through plastic teeth. There are several more neighbours we know by sight or by nickname: Kate the Miller, Long Tom, Pratie Gallagher, Scissors Flynn, Pat the Blower and Pat the Twin. Wiry country women wearing belted raincoats and cotton headscarves with watchful expressions sit alongside husbands on their best behaviour dressed in suits and fawn cardigans, with topcoats and felt hats, and talking amongst themselves about airlocks and shorthorns.

"You're late on it today," my mother says to a neighbour, and they start to chat as soon as she takes her seat. Everyone who boards the bus is brought into the conversation.

"You have the umbrella with you, Mary?"

"They were giving out rain on the radio."

"You're looking as fit as a fiddle, Jimmy."

"I could kiss me toes if I had me socks off."

A flock of smooth-faced women with coiled barbed-wire-tight home perms, good winter coats and holding fur-lined gloves gabble loud as turkeys.

The bus makes slow progress up through the gears but never makes any speed. It is either delayed behind a slow car driven at twenty-five miles an hour by a little man looking out through the steering wheel, or a tractor with baled hay and a bucket of calf-nuts in the transport box. Then we need to stop to leave the papers off at every post office, and again at Geevagh, Conway's and Tailor's crossroads. It is a full hour and a half before we reach the blue outskirts of the town.

The town lights stay lit all day in the deep gloom of December. We get off at the traffic lights on the Mail Coach road and take a short-cut into the centre. On the terraced hill above us we can see men out in their tiny front gardens, smoking cigarettes and waiting for the shopping wives to come home. Church spires loom through the blanket of coal smoke and near-freezing fog. The streets are netted with coloured bulbs, and the windscreens are only half-cleared on the snow-capped cars down from the mountain.

"Where do you want to go first, Mammy?"

"We'll go to the hardware."

"Do you not want to shop for clothes?"

"Why don't we look in the Market Yard?"

Ringed close about our mother we plot the day ahead as she opens her purse and looks at her money again.

"We'll stay with you, Mammy," I tell her, "until you get the shopping done."

And we trail her about the shops, my younger brother adding unwanted items to her shopping basket: cooking chocolate, sandwich spread, a box of Dream Topping.

"We don't need all that," Mammy says. "And put that bottle back and get me a smaller one."

She keeps us distracted roving the supermarket aisles finding the essential items on her list: tin foil, packets of jelly and sponges for the trifle. But she has made it clear we don't want to buy all our wants here, where, she says, they would stand over you looking for the last penny. The turkey, the ham, the bread, the milk, the eggs and loose rashers needed to tide us over the holiday when the shops are closed, we will buy from the local shopkeeper, who always gives his regular clients a Christmas box of a cake, leaf tea and cigarettes.

Between shops, the Christmas crowd elbow and jostle around each other on the packed streets, with almost everybody clutching a brace of plastic supermarket bags with dodgy bottoms, the sides worn ragged by the extra boxes of every shape and size in bright wrapping paper. We bump into a street sweeper staggering home after Christmas drinks. Children mess with the headlights while waiting inside heavily loaded parked cars outside the supermarkets. A perished young lad minds the Christmas trees for sale on a windy corner. Tinker children are out and about selling bunches of holly. The shop windows are packed with seasonal biscuit boxes and tea-caddies, rich chocolate liqueurs, boxes of cards and tinsel decorations, fairy lights and fake snow sprayed from aerosol cans on glass panes latticed with red insulating tape. An unconvincing cotton-wool-bearded Santy wearing farmer's black wellington boot sits in a red crêpe paper-covered booth in one of the shops, charging for every visit. The enticements to spend are everywhere.

We stop only for the carol singers in the arcade, led by a bearded man with a guitar. Dropping a coin into the collector's rattling can we have a recitation from memory ready:

*"Christmas is coming and the geese are getting fat*
*Will you please put a penny in the old man's hat*
*If you haven't got a penny, then a halfpenny will do*
*If you haven't got a halfpenny, then God bless you."*

In the toy shop chubby children in hooded coats run wild amongst the displays in a way we would never be allowed. They open boxes, drag down stuffed toys, battery-driven and spring-wound things and leave them scattered about the shop floor.

"This is what Santy is bringing me," one shrills.

We get to pick out one special want; a junior magician kit, an Airfix model aircraft or a chemistry set, books, jigsaws, colouring pencil sets.

"They have me robbed," my mother says to a passing schoolmaster from home.

"Anything that's educational," he says.

And as we have a high-gain aerial and can pick up the English channels from Enniskillen I take charge of buying the bumper double issues of the *Radio Times* and *TV Times* with what's on television over the Christmas.

We have tea and a warm-up and then get back to the shopping, sharing out the bags to carry between us as we make it back to the bus ahead of time. We sit watching the stragglers take their seats or stop and stand awhile beside the partition talking to the driver. Then a wild-eyed woman with bright red hair arrives. She keeps changing seats until she is sitting next to us. She smells of whiskey and carries an exotic looking pot plant.

"There was a little Mexican boy who cried all night because he had no present to give to the baby Jesus," she explains with teary eyes to my anxious younger brother. "But when he got up in the morning the leaves of the green hedge outside his front door had miraculously turned a beautiful red, just like flowers, and ever since the poinsettia has grown wild in Mexico."

Everyone makes a path for her between the shopping bags when she stumbles off the bus making her way home alone clutching her precious poinsettia.

The skies are clear beyond the lit bus windows: a promise of frost in the pastel dusk. Crows roost high in the sycamores. Cattle on a bare hillside follow a man with a load of fodder tied in a rope carried on his back.

We step off the bus into the dark and walk the last part home, stopping at the stile where we left our wellington boots in the morning. Then we take a short-cut through the fields, carting the shopping bags and careful not to drop our messages. I see the light of our kitchen window up ahead. There is a sweet old world smell of hay on the cold air in the farmyard. And we find Daddy in his socks with his feet up by the fire, the outside jobs done. He has a mutton chop stewing for himself in a pot. Another pot of spuds stands freshly boiled, waiting for the mince and beans in our shopping bag to make a handy supper.

Having burst into the quiet house we start taking everything out of the bags. There are cylinders of mixed spice, cinnamon, ginger and mixed peel, raisins and sultanas and a new mixing bowl for the Christmas pudding. And even Mammy is in a rush to show Daddy the presents bought for relations and the children of her closest neighbours: toilet sets, children's bright woolly things, ankle-socks, face-cloths, story books, comics, tidy boxes of chocolates.

"They'll do grand," Daddy says, glossing over the presents. "Did you remember to get cigarettes?"

We have our own parcels to stash away in the bedroom. The tree isn't up yet and there is no tradition of leaving presents under the tree in our house. We will have the little gifts, the milk chocolates, the pairs of socks, the paperback books and ornaments we bought on the quiet today ready to hand over on Christmas Day. And now as soon as we have changed out of the good clothes we wore to town, we separate the gifts out on the quilt and search the house for clear tape and a roving scissors to cut and make the wrapping paper go round.

We are as restless as bluebottles in a fish shop after our day out, but we do our level best to keep up this peaceful atmosphere in the house by helping Mammy with the late supper. Later, Daddy sits in his armchair with one leg gathered up under him, and we form a ring around the fire, our presents put away, the big day's shopping done and the spending fever broken.

Though tolerant towards our heightened expectations, Daddy is slow to demonstrate the right attitude to Christmas. He seems removed from our excitement, unconcerned by the build-up. He has for instance already eaten a slice from the Christmas cake before the holiday. And he has torn a bottle of stout out of the six-pack we bought in town, and opened the visitors' whiskey before we've had any visitors. Last year, when even my younger brother was old enough to notice, he cut two pine branches, tied them together with string and told us it was a Christmas tree.

So this year I am taking it on myself to get the Christmas tree: or I should say, to hike to the plantation on the mountain to steal a tree.

First, though, I go looking for holly. As soon as the late December rain lets up I head out across the hill fields with our two dogs, the collie and the terrier, at my heels. The ground is soft with the colour gone from the old grass where hungry pheasants have left their scrapings in the dead bracken. I carry a bow-saw with the handle over my shoulder, snug as a rifle strap.

Crawling through a hole in the hedge that marins our neighbour's farm, I press on knowing a good holly tree two fields away. Other holly trees have either no berries to show at all or have berries some years only; but this grand holly tree never disappoints. Though not on our land it has the best berries around, even if they grow right at the top, and I have to climb up through a dense screen of prickly green holly leaves to get to them. There are stubs of cut branches from previous raids, and spurred on by the success of other years I make it to the top and gladly witness the saw-blade bite into silver bark and see fresh white sawdust carried away on the breeze. Then there is a satisfying snap as the heavy red-berried branch breaks and falls cleanly and hits the ground below with a solid thud.

After I proudly drag the big branch home with its cargo of berries intact, I face into a watery winter evening sunset as the low sun punches a hole in the clouds. Night has fallen and the blackbirds are on their way to bed by the time I reach the mountain plantation. The dogs whine to be lifted over the sheep-wire fencing around the plantation. Once inside the fence the feeling of transgression is strong, but I search the lines of trees for a nicely rounded young Norway spruce. And I feel like Christmas has truly arrived when I smell the fresh pine-resin from the newly cut down shapely conifer that I've chosen.

It is fully dark by the time I get back, tired and happy to have met no-one while on my secret business. I leave the tree outside and go around the house until there are sprigs of richly berried holly over the pictures and the window frames of every room. The holly is meant to safeguard the house and I take care to see the job is done right.

Outside the front door I stand the tree in a galvanized bucket using gravel and stones. Daddy moves between the cow-sheds and calves' barns with the newer buckets full of fresh milk, while I manhandle the tree by myself into the front room, and then cut stray branches down to size with the hedge clippers. It takes careful balancing to make the tree stay upright, and it is only when I have the tree properly anchored that I find the decorations in a cardboard box kept under the bed. We have a set of frosted glass bulbs my mother said cost a lot at the time they were bought, but have worked every year since without fail, and once the loose bulbs are tightened in their sockets the string of lights springs on.

The swags of tinsel are starting to go bald in places and many of the baubles are chipped but the overall effect is still lovely when the tree is decorated and the bulbs lighted.

This is my favourite moment, a moment more precious than Christmas Day itself: sitting with the table-lamp off and only the flames from the open fire and the lights on the Christmas tree to colour the room. The dogs sleep on the rug and the greenwood forest smell fills the room. And a short while later the idea of peace and plenty in the world seems so real, so close at hand, drinking a cup of tea and eating from the tin of USA assorted biscuits with a nice Christmas tree in place.

Our postman is a clean-shaven, well-kept bachelor who lives with an unmarried brother and loves a chat with the housewives. He brings increasing numbers of Christmas cards in the canvas sack that hangs from his shoulder on each of the closing days to Christmas, including Saturdays. When the cards come out of his sack I think it a shame to blemish and tear open the spotless envelopes. And the envelopes themselves are done up in tight bundles for each townland, held together with fat elastic bands. Our postman is extremely careful sorting the bundles, licking the top of his thumb as he goes through the tightly stacked envelopes like a man dealing from a deck of playing cards.

"A cup of tea, James?" my mother offers.

"I'll have a drop in me hand." he says.

Then he reaches deep into his canvas sack and brings out a card for my mother from her sister in America. It comes every year without fail: an especially bright card with a cheque inside made out in dollars. The postman smiles when he leaves this card with its airmail markings on the envelope on the top of the bunch on the sideboard. And as it is Christmas Eve my mother gives him tea in a good willow pattern cup and saucer, with a thick slice of Christmas cake on a side-plate, together with a glass of neat whiskey.

"Good health and a happy Christmas to you, ma'am," he says, his peaked cap balanced on his blue-uniformed knee.

It is his reward for bringing our letters and creamery cheques all year; for waiting in the kitchen while my mother sits down to finish another letter for him to post; for taking messages and animal medicines between my mother and her sister who lives in the next townland; for telling us we have cattle out on the road; for letting us know that a removal is at seven, or a funeral on Friday morning after the eleven o'clock mass, and finally for being the one to make certain all of our childhood letters got posted in good time to Santy at the North Pole.

When he has finished his tea and whiskey and Christmas cake he lilts a tune and then he walks up the lane to where the ground levels out, settles his sack of letters over his shoulder, takes a firm hold of the handlebars of his push-bike and away he goes into history.

Early on Christmas night Daddy is shunted out of the house and off to the pub to get out of the way of mother and children. In the fellowship of the other outcasts from the busy home kitchens of the valley he takes his Christmas drink in the front bar. And then he stays on a while, buying extra-generous rounds; spending a bit.

The darkness lies thick as a horse-blanket against the window-panes. But the 100 watt bulb burns brightly in the middle of the ceiling in our kitchen. Swags of Christmas cards hang on a string on the end wall; Victorian gentlemen in black top-hats, winter singing robins amidst sprays of silver glitter, coach-and-four carriages and women wearing tied hats, bustles and ribbons. Snowflakes. Candles. Pine-cones. The trappings of the perfect Christmas.

At the kitchen table we are Mammy's perfectly behaved helpers, looking for small jobs to do and mixing bowls to lick. We help her to carry in the enormous, white, goose-pimpled turkey to remove the giblets and get it ready for stuffing. The kettle is steaming and there is a big pot simmering on the black hob. The plum pudding is wrapped in pudding cloth and sits in a double saucepan. Breadcrumbs tumble out of the metal grater. There is also a round of ham to be boiled, then roasted in the oven tomorrow and given a glaze of brown sugar and cloves. We are a last-minute-with-everything family; and with one cake already half-eaten, Mammy has to ice another cake, so we have blocks of almond marzipan to soften into a roll and fine icing sugar to moisten and blend. My brother and I tussle in complete silence over who should be in charge of the little plastic figures used year-in and year-out, propped up in the fresh icing to decorate the top of the cake.

If we have to go to the back door to throw tea-leaves in the hedge we can hear in the still yard the farm animals making tranquil sounds chewing on their fodder as they lie down in the Bethlehem of our barns. Our mother has said it isn't safe to put candles in the windows all night - to light the holy family on their journey; too many fires have started that way. But every electric light in the house is left on, and standing at the back door we can see the hills full of lights, our whole townland and the distant countryside brightly lit up. Above our heads the stars are winking Christmas candles. Venus shines over the shoulder of the mountain like the guiding star in the East. The warm, spicy air from the kitchen is a premonition of wise Kings bringing strange and exotic gifts of gold, frankincense and myrrh to the baby Jesus. And the water in the winter drains tinkles like the jingle of bells announcing a timeless mystery.

The Christmas promise is even more intense when an older brother buttons up his coat to go to the midnight chapel. It is not that long ago since we would refuse to go to bed on Christmas night only we knew Santy was coming and bold children might get overlooked. We were past that now, but still close enough in time to be touched by the sensation of those bygone Christmas nights when we lay awake and watched the steady moonlight at the end of the bed until we heard the men coming back again from midnight mass, talking and drinking soup in the kitchen.

We had a plate of biscuits and a glass of orange juice left out for Santy we hoped nobody downstairs would disturb. And at some hour of this magical night Santy would creep mysterious, and just a little frightening, into the bedroom where we had tried so hard but failed to stay awake; if only to hear the magical hoof-tap and harness-jingle of the flying reindeer on the ridge-tiles of our roof, or the rustle of soot in the chimney. It never happened, and Santy was never caught out. For years he filled us with a sense of never-to-be-matched anticipation. And we woke each year in a state of pure delight to find what we'd asked for at the foot of the bed on Christmas morning.

Over the years we pounced on gifts of FBI suction dart-guns, spud-guns and water pistols, and metal German Lugers that were black, detailed and deadly. Especially prized were the Dinky and Matchbox brand model cars with doors and bonnets that actually opened. One year I got a huge bag of green plastic soldiers manfully posed with rifles and rocket-launchers and radio backpacks, but the whole platoon was eventually left limbless and chewed to pieces - not by the machinery of war, but by a new terrier pup. There were unasked for add-ons too such as building blocks and jigsaw puzzles, paint boxes and colouring books, soon abandoned in the hullabaloo of cap-guns that devoured red paper rolls dotted with bumps of reeking gunpowder.

Soon after waking up the household on Christmas morning we headed off out the fields in our new vinyl cowboy hats and sheriff's badges, half-dressed but strapped into holsters and pistols and carrying Winchester rifles with enough firepower to rout King Kong out of the lower fields.

No callers are wanted at the house on Christmas Day. We scrub and dress for first mass to be home early to start the dinner. After a clear cold night, motorists have kettles full of hot water needed to defrost locks and clear windshields and side windows. We take our seats in the perishing cold chapel and sit out a long sermon looking over at the infant Jesus with no clothes in the crib in the chilly cross-house.

We tuck into a hearty Christmas morning fry-up as soon as we get home, and then we clean the ashes out of the grate and leave the fire set in the front room. Everyone is anxious to guarantee the smooth running of the day. The cattle are reluctant to go far after they are turned out of the barns for the few short hours of light, while old bedding is mucked out of the barns and fresh fodder left in its place. I chop logs to work up an appetite for the dinner. Soldiers' requests are played on the radio and I tick off films and favourite programmes in the double-edition television guides.

There are sprouts to be peeled and boiled, and cream to be whipped for the plum pudding and trifle. And Daddy has to be talked into wearing his good suit after he has the outside jobs done.

"Don't be making such a fuss," he says.

But the real fuss is reserved for the turkey. Getting the heat up in the cast iron black Stanley range, polished brightly for the day that's in it, is an art and science best left to my mother. The fire needs extra loadings of coal, measured to keep the roasting temperature steady. And measured too amongst my mother's calculations is the turkey weight balanced with the number of hours needed in the oven. Too much heat and the meat will be too dry; too little and the flesh inside the leg will stay pink and undercooked. And throughout the bird takes constant basting in its juices.

There is a tussle over whose turn it is to make the brandy butter. And someone has to stand over the big cauldron of boiling potatoes to watch for the skins to burst open.

"Lift and drain them the minute they start laughing," Mammy says.

"There's not a smile out of them yet," Daddy says, testing with a fork.

The extra leaf is opened out on the table, and by three o'clock we are ready to sit down to dinner, even if it means we have to leave off watching Billy Smart's Circus.

"Is the turkey all right? I think the breast is too dry," Mammy says as she serves up the dinner on the biggest plates we have in the house.

"It's lovely," we say in unison.

It does not matter to us if the turkey meat is either too pink or too dry. What is important is the array of familiar tastes of our traditional Christmas dinner: the turkey breast or brown meat on the leg with bread stuffing, the brassy taste of Brussels sprouts, gravy and brown sauce, the homemade brandy butter on the pudding, the custard topping on the trifle, and tea and Christmas cake with white icing and yellow marzipan to round out the feast.

Before long it is dark outside. The cattle are back in the barns, and everybody is stretched out in the front room, brazed and half-asleep in front of the television. Though we can hardly touch another thing, a box of Milk Tray chocolates is opened to relieve the sense of anticlimax. After all the effort and the anticipation Christmas Day is over and done with for another year.

"You won't find Christmas coming round again," Daddy says to tease us, and we all belly-groan in his direction.

Later in the evening we go to visit a school friend's house to take a hand in a family game of cards. Games of twenty-five are played for small coins. And the turkey carcass is stripped for sandwiches.

On Saint Stephen's Day we dress up as wren-boys and go the rounds of the roads. The cowboy hats and Lone Ranger masks come in useful. And we make our masked arrival in long coats from American parcels. Thinly disguised, with my perished hands holding a tin whistle on which I can barely manage to play Silent Night and

The Dawning of the Day, I arrive at a farmhouse door where a small child shouts: "Mammy, Mammy, the ramble boys are here."

Along with my brothers I begin my tuneless busking, and it is a relief to everybody when the money drops into the Cocoa tin with the slot cut in the top and we immediately move on.

By New Year's Eve there is a lace of snow on the ground. Daddy steps outside with the shotgun. He fires two shots into the air. More gun-shots echo about the valley at the stroke of midnight, as coalminers outsider their homes fire into the bushes to frighten off misfortune over the coming year.

We celebrate New Year watching Andy Stewart on the television celebrate Hogmanay. Then first thing in the morning on New Year's Day I hang a new calendar on the nail, and set out in the falling wet snowflakes. I have houses to visit where it is still considered unlucky to have a red-headed stranger for a first caller. My hair is dark and I am brought into council row cottages and two-storey farmhouses alike, where I am treated to tea and biscuits, lemonade, and have money pressed into my hand. Like the holly over the door, the fairy lights on the pine tree, the shots fired on the street, here is another charm meant to hold the family together.

There is a cock-step in the days after Little Christmas on the 6th of January and a thaw has turned the snow to water. The family box of milk chocolates is long eaten and New Year resolutions have melted away like the snowmen with nuggets of Arigna coal for eyes.

It was in school in the run-up to Christmas one year that the rumours and doubts about Santy arose. Suspicions were cast on flying reindeer and letters posted to the North Pole.

"There's no such thing as Santy."

"Yes, there is."

"No, there isn't."

"Prove it."

After a top-to-bottom search of the house I came to the wardrobe in Mammy and Daddy's room. Standing on a chair I looked in over the top and my heart cracked open at the sight of the toys on my wish-list to Santy.

I said nothing to my parents or my little brother. But that unwanted revelation led to the discovery of a world where presents were ordered with down payments weeks in advance, left safely aside in the shops, and finally hidden in the house by Daddy – often on the very day when we went to town on the bus. Daddy had been on a different mission while we were out. And he was the one who crept unseen every Christmas into our bedroom in his socks and left the presents on the dressing table or at the foot of the bed for us to find in the morning.

I began to understand something about my parents then; how they worked their own magic to hold the house together. The care and trouble they took to meet our needs, to see we were nourished, secure and loved.

Every year our needs were discovered early and the letters we wrote to Santy held back by our postman on his bicycle. We were never without a fresh turkey and pudding and cake for the festive table, and on shopping trips into town, ends were made to meet. So if there was the pain of losing Santy, there was the comfort of finding a different Father Christmas. A man who worked hard to provide for us, but hid his feelings as successfully as Santy hide our toys until we were fast asleep. And when it was all out in the open I had to promise not to spoil the Christmas magic for others younger than me. That sense of permanence and security, of family love and togetherness and gifts conjured out of nowhere. It was my first big adult secret: keeping that Christmas promise.

# A GOOD ONE

IT WAS A TIME WHEN only a bona fide traveller could buy drink on a Sunday. And the bicycle riding constabulary, using white imperial measuring tapes on spools that were made to read the width of the road at the scenes of traffic accidents and collisions, took the measure of the journey from the end of your bed to the brass foot-rail of the bar counter. Less than three miles between the two locations and you had no legal right to spring the arm of the bell over the door of a drinking premises, nor leave your money down on the wood.

The last Sunday in the month of July, Garland Sunday. A day, by tradition, when good people went to mass up in the mountains. A day when country priests stood over lichen-circled mass rocks in the heather, and the worshippers made Sunday outings along the bracken paths to gather on the breezy crests of the summer hills. A day when more adventurous pilgrims brought sturdy sticks for the reek, and went barefoot and fasting up the scree paths and slopes of the holy mountain, Croagh Patrick.

Tom Packie is up an hour when he feels his famous thirst bettering his devotion. With the split sections of a traditional wooden flute, locally known as his three-piece wallet, snug in the inside pocket of his good suit jacket he walks the mile or so into town looking for a *seisiún*. He meets a crowd of people on the sunny pavement and stops to talk to a pilgrim neighbour, queuing for the bus to Croagh Patrick. Then he crosses the street to Murray's public house and walks casually past the front door, double-bolted between the holy hours from two until four o'clock. He goes around to a brown side-door with the words Wines and Spirits printed in gold leaf on the narrow pane of glass above the lintel.

"Tom Packie," says a blue-uniformed sergeant, appearing out of the shadowy door of the whitewashed outhouse, where the publican kept his winter turf and bottled and corked his stout out of the brewery kegs. "Are you not going to the reek today?"

"No," says Tom Packie. "But I was going to knock."

# CLOUDBURST

THE DRUIDS FELT IT WAS on the edge of water that poetry was revealed to them. And from the gable window of an upstairs bedroom of our house on the mountain, like an eye looking out onto the world, I could always see the serpent bends of the local river on its journey around the valley: a black river under grey skies, a silver river in summer sunlight, a pure blue river in the springtime and a brown river in full spate.

I must have been about eleven or twelve years old when, after a restless night, I went to the gable window and opened the curtains. For the whole of the previous day and all through the night the rain had drummed a steady tattoo on the slate roof of our two-storey farmhouse. The night had been full of the sound of eave-runs spilling into skillet pots and rain-barrels.

It was still raining as I looked out and saw my father bringing in the brow-beaten cattle for milking, their big-muscled thighs pulling their hooves with a sucking sound out of the soft mud in the gaps, the cow-tracks immediately filling up with water.

When I went outside in my anorak I could feel the brooding, elemental force of the saturated hills, and sense a mysterious significance in the blurring of the boundary between the upward thrust of the mountain and the wheeling, featureless cloud concealing the crest.

In my coat and wellingtons I made for the low hills, to see the torrents filling the drains and culverts, and the peat-tinted flood tumbling into the gullies.

At the cloud-line I entered a wet blanketing greyness stretching to the mountain conifer plantations. I looked into familiar foxholes and crevices, and checked to see if the sweat-houses were still standing; if the lintel stones of the abandoned homesteads had fallen, if the thatched turf-stacks sheltering vermin-covered bumble-bees had taken in water. To see if the monument stones, heather stretches, turf-banks, sphagnum moss and nesting grouse, old quarry faces and closed mine shafts had not been washed away.

Then dropping back down again out of the fog I noted the flood rising quickly in the valley, the riverbanks on the brink of bursting, the outlines of the river already lost under water spreading out across the fields.

Men with land at the river were moving their cattle to higher ground. And back at the house where I needed to dry off I found my grandfather opening the front panel of the coal-burning range to combat the damp air. He saw me in my wellingtons and looking at his own brown Polish leather boots he said, "I wonder if these new boots are waterproof?"

"It's fireproof boots you'd need," my father said, going back to his outside jobs in the rain.

Looking out the gable window once more I could see the river grown to twice its size. And I had the urge to get back out there. To task the elements. So I headed out into the rain with our fox terrier for company and reassurance, to witness the mud and wash of the day, to wade through waist-high rushes getting my jeans darkly drenched up to my thighs .

Scrambling up the embankment I reached the railroad: a narrow-gauge line dismantled before my time. Its rusting safety notices were still bolted to the original wrought iron gates, but the level cinder-bed track had thickets of sloe-bearing blackthorn growing there now; fairy-tale deep thorny patches where badgers had their straw beds drying in the mouth of their setts.

I followed the track to reach the concrete footbridge we called the 'Balk'. The river looked like it would soon cross the bridge and floodwater was starting to pool where the path met the bridge, but I waded in, feeling the weight and pressure of the cold water press against my rubber boots, hoping a cold spill wouldn't cross the tops.

On warm summer days this was a lovely part of the river to visit; a place where cleg-pestered cattle would stand knee-deep in the water, where kingfishers swept past in a lighting flash of blue plumage; a place where you could measure the subtle changes in the shape of the river's black sandy islands and deltas; a place where the egg-shell brittle stems of clay pipes, biscuit-brown clay jars and coloured bits of crockery, old remedy bottles with names printed in the glass washed up as keepsakes.

This part of the river-bank was also the site of boy-gang meetings after school for the building of stepping stone bridges and rickety rafts, which we launched at the shallow fording places. And a short distance further downriver from the bridge there was a deep turn-hole where we fished for trout with fat worms kept in jam-jars; where we spent hours skipping flat stones across the water, where we floated bottles on the current and hunted them down with stones in fierce competition, our vandal instincts appeased.

We knew the locations of all of the bridges too hidden under the overgrown railway track. Some were low and dark and uninviting. But there was one bridge built to accommodate a major stream with decent headroom. You bowed your head and entered its low, dark mouth and felt spider-webs tickle your face and imagined bats hanging in the shadows waiting to get caught in your hair. But going through the eye of the bridge was a rite of passage from which you emerged into virgin banks of vivid yellow gorse and fleecy white clouds in a blue sky and saw it all from another standpoint.

Now, after I made my way safely onto the bridge I stood watching the river from another angle, alive to the titanic force of the swiftly moving brown and white foam-flecked deluge. The flood had carried a dead tree as far as the bridge, and the whole structure vibrated with the power of the water rushing between the pillars where the limbs of the dead tree had lodged and formed a partial blockage and concentrated its force. Standing as a witness to the moving borders and power of the flood I knew how foolish and yet important it was for me to be there to survey and register what I found, taking the measure of my own courage with the first lines of something approaching poetry forming on my tongue.

# PRACTICAL ROOMS & PREFABS

WE WERE THE CHILDREN of farmers and coalminers, factory workers and labourers; the horny-handed sons of the soil and daughters of the daub. And we burst like a landslide through the front door of the nearest Vocational School thanks to Donna O' Malley's announcement in the Dail that from 1969 onwards all schools up to Intermediate Certificate level would be free and that free buses would bring students from rural areas to the nearest school.

At the time, the biggest gathering of young people all week happened after mass on Sundays. Weekdays were passed in a brutalised daze having your hands reddened with the rod in the three-room National School or desperately trying to stay invisible from the teacher while sucking on the top of a pencil like it was the salmon of knowledge

Now and then we had visiting magicians who spilled coins from their sleeves or a touring animal show that stopped outside the National school yard on an open lorry; with scrofulous rabbits, one-eyed bantam cocks, gerbils that might have been shrunken rats and sad, wet-eyed hamsters. And there was a day each year when we dipped our plastic combs under the tap, cat-licked and smartened ourselves up for the school photographer.

The Vocational School looked and felt different. Bisected by a central entrance, the main building had a long corridor where the girls kept to the Kitchen, Science Room, Shorthand and Commerce side of the building and the boys occupied the opposite Woodwork and Metalwork Room end.

On my first day a schoolfellow called Gerry Regan had possibly the shortest induction on record. It began with a hunt for chairs, a delaying tactic beloved of every generation of students who ever passed through the school; this business of wandering between the prefabs at the start of every class to shave a few minutes off your captivity.

As soon as we were settled the Principal gave us a pep talk and told us to keep our noses to the grindstone, and 'A good education is easily carried'. Then Mr Toner, the English teacher presided over the induction, which was really a form filling exercise. This, being September, there was also a wasp in the room. So the first thing Gerry Regan did was roll up his form and swipe at the wasp. The cylinder of paper connected with the wasp and lobbed the insect directly into Mr Toner's sideburn where it got stuck as he roared at Gerry to 'get out and stay out'.

By the early 1970s the number of students had increased to the extent that even the additional wooden prefabs surrounding the practical rooms of the main building were heavily over-crowded. And it was out amongst the prefabs I struggled to master compulsory Irish taught by Mrs Caulfield who gave me *Peig* to read - a record of the hardships and misfortunes suffered by a woman who struck me as a terrible drudge whose only comfort in life was following coffins to the graveyard.

"*Amadan!*" was a word frequently applied, not by our Irish but by our Maths teacher. She must have been younger, but to my eyes she seemed about eighty years old or more with her snow-white head and a constant cigarette going in the classroom. She mauled us through higher mathematics; physically twisting students' ears to haul unwilling brains over Pythagoras's theorem, which she called the bridge of asses: a living terror to us all, and not a sign of her to retire; square-rooted in simultaneous equations and the binomial theorem to the last of her days.

As nearly every town in Ireland had a bacon factory and a tannery I soon learned that when the Geography teacher asked what a certain province produced the safe answer was always, "Shoes, grass and molasses, Sir'.

Just as important to remember was to equip myself with a T-square on days when we had Mechanical Drawing and Building

Construction classes. And by and large my school days were orderly and dull and heavily loaded with homework.

The only real 'doss' or let-off was Father Logan's Religion class. Father Logan was a short, stout, frog-faced man with a heavy topcoat, shiny shoes and a warm, unchristian car on rainy evenings. His religion class was compulsory and to pass the time we tormented him with daft questions.

"Father, if God is all-powerful could he build a fence so high he couldn't jump over it?"

"Could he make a rock so big he couldn't lift it?"

Often we just folded our arms and glared as he passed out Good News Catechism books with pen-and-ink drawings that fell short of their aspiration to make religion trendy. In fact the dodgy illustrations prompted me to draw my own cartoon figure of Jesus on the edge of every page where he ascended into orbit as you flicked the pages past your thumb. At the end of the Ascension sequence I put a caption in a balloon over one of the apostles saying: "Gentlemen, we have lift-off."

Between the over-crowded prefabs were the volleyball court and a garden and a lower court under whose bare block walls the smokers congregated. The Mayflower Ballroom was only a stone's throw away – but all hell broke loose if a window got broken.

The gable end of the metalwork room allowed for endless games of handball and wet days meant queues for table tennis if the ball wasn't lost or dented. Our school was big on volleyball with football relegated to a swampy field at a distance from the school where I was taught to use surveyor's poles and chains to measure for the umpteenth time that sodden spratty acre that passed for a playing field.

There was a coal-fired boiler house policed by the school Caretaker, often seen in the corridor with a shovel full of hot cinders to get the cookers going in the kitchen. Since the Caretaker was thought to carry stories back to the teachers we reckoned his birthday fell on Spy Wednesday.

Along with the search for chairs and killing wasps there were several more hand-me-down traditions that included countless hours spent sitting on the storage heaters, copying homework on the bus, filling Fr. Logan's hat with chalk dust, getting someone to look up the chimney of the forge in the metalwork room and then hitting the hood to cover them in soot.

On fair days you might get held back from school to run ahead of cattle and stop them breaking through gaps as they were walked into town. And sometimes an older student might come back after lunch tipsy from the bargain making, or Winne Ward could arrive looking for the price of the drink she'd been promised by lads out to cause a commotion.

If for some reason I ever found myself on the outside in the silent grounds of the school while everyone else was at work indoors it made me feel strange, uncomfortably removed, and conscious of my own absence from the true purpose of the place.

Being asthmatic and having a dismal attendance record I was forever trying to catch up. But recognising how much I loved the science room with its Belfast sinks and Bunsen burner valves and chemical cupboard the Science and Biology teacher, and self-styled rabbit-skinner and frog-dissector, Mr Boland would greet my hot-cheeked return saying, "Were you the Francis Farrelly I met so long ago, in the bog below Belmullet, in the County of Mayo?"

I liked Mr Boland, though I knew he had to be avoided when he ducked past the Principal's office with a Monday pink face. Down the corridor he'd lope, a textbook under his arm rolled tight as a military baton as he entered into the reek of science-room chemicals.

The commotion would die away as we took up our places along the benches, toying with the hope of a butane gas explosion. Mr Boland seated himself behind a large, raised desk, litmus paper dry in the mouth, among retort stands, tripods and test-tubes, incubating his hangover.

"Higgins."

"Yes, sir."

"Report."

"Yes, sir."

"Parts of the digestive system."

"Moran."

"Yes, sir."

"Report."

"Yes, sir."

"Peristalsis."

"Prick," said a disgruntled voice from the back.

Tommy "the trout" Higgins was then brought to the blackboard to sketch and label a diagram of the pancreas, stomach and duodenum, done in coloured chalk. Every drawing was copied straight out of the Folens' textbook, traced on to the blackboard, copied into the graph paper side of our science exercise books, and then safely forgotten. We'd sit there writing all day, longing for practical experiments with dangerous chemical salts and battery acids, boiling liquids, hydrogen explosions in lidded gas jars and disgraceful operations on frogs.

"Quiet down the back," Mr Boland would shout, and our scribbling would start up again.

Mr Boland was also an amateur boxing coach, and when he had an eye to sport he'd improvise a ring in the lower end of the room where the hard lads and braggarts could spar and jab and scuffle. After school he'd motor his aspiring Mohammed Alis in an overloaded yellow Austin to county boxing club matches. The Mountain Mauler versus Scrap Iron. With Scrap Iron, our school bully, landing back black-eyed and sullen after a first round trouncing. And Mr Boland barking at him: "Join the art class, McGinley, if you're that fond of the canvas."

I was happiest in the science room but liked woodwork too, marking waste timber with xxxxx and secretly drawing the same Xs on the back of someone's jacket. The room had a sweet pine resin smell from sawing the lengths of 2x4 white deal we cut down to project sized pieces using a tenon-saw under Mr McGloin's direction to 'measure twice and cut once'.

The metalwork room reeked of the green Swarfega soap we used to clean our hands under the stern direction of Mr Coggins whose severity in fact miraculously kept us from getting mangled by the industrial lathes and metal shears we learned to operate in his workshop. The double-classes passed quickly in the reek of solder and flux and grease, starting with each man making a raid on the next locker down the line to make up a full kit of tools - metal punch, hammer, file and square, with Gerry Regan, the last man in the line often found locked inside the store-room.

And then there was Mr Toner's English class, full of long-faced lads of fourteen, already able dealers at the cattle and sheep marts, and girls only waiting to get nursing or find a job in the bank, ploughing through adverbs and pronouns while having their lunches stolen, their flasks broken and their bags smuggled out the window. On my school report the English teacher wrote: "Could do better"; under which I wrote: "Could do worse".

There are longed-for half-days and the prospect of disruption due to snow. But just when you arrive in class on a snowy morning and think that attendance is so small the school is bound to close, lads like Gerry Regan who've been absent all year showed up; and any hopes you had are dashed that the headmaster will call the bus drivers to say the school is closing early. For Gerry of course he was probably trying to avoid the extra work on the farm at home on account of the snow.

Trips outside the school were rare but we had a few educational outings, chiefly to the sugar factory in Tuam or the turbine hall in the Arigna power station, though one far-sighted trip included a visit to the Pulse electronic company in Galway and an encounter with the climate controlled room where they operated impressive banks of the first computers I'd ever seen.

The highlight though was the school tour to the Spring show in the RDS. And just as there was no joy in being at large in the school grounds with the teachers and pupils alike busily at work, so it was always better to be on the annual school tour rather than take the day off.

The school tour let you see your teachers as people in their own right, and while we could be barefaced brats, we kept to the general rule that no student should return from the school tour drunker than the teachers; though in fact it was mostly a harmless can or two of shandy we shared around in the same spirit of transgression that saw couples pairing off at the back of the bus to engage in hand-holding under a coat or sweet first kisses and light petting on the return journey in the dark.

No such intimacy was allowed on the big yellow 45-seater school buses that took me round the country on the twice daily journey too and from the 'Tech'. To our constant disappointment, the greatest freeze or blizzard could not stop these chunky yellow buses from showing up, as the radio on dark and filthy wet winter mornings mocked us with inducements to "Join the JWT set" on Joe Walsh Tours new package holiday escapes to the sun.

In the evenings on the back seat, bouncing over the bog roads for hours at a stretch, I passed the farmsteads and the laneways, the roadside homes and the county council cottages, the birthplaces and the stomping grounds of my friends and classmates, looking on at the passing countryside through grimy windows at Fenagh and Keshcarrigan, Acres Lake, the Tinker's Cross and the Wooden Bridge, Molly Logan's, Knockvicar, Bridgecartron, Ballyfarnon, Keadue and Arigna. Generation upon generation of scholars collected and dropped off throughout the vocational school year each at their own particular crossroads; with each carrying their schoolbag and a green Córas Iompair Éireann free transport ticket like a passport, coming home to parents who looked on proudly at their school-going sons and daughters and saw us as a wonderment. Changed. Fortunate. Knowledgeable.

# ON THE MARKET

IT IS A WICKEDLY COLD, windy Tuesday in January. The skies are leaden, the streets bleak and cruel. The windows and doors of the small town are tightly closed. No shop will open before ten; and then, only for the odd smoker, gasping for a cigarette and eager for the headlines and obituaries of the morning paper. A tractor rolls through town and a cow bellows into the dreaming bedrooms, to announce the first mart of the New Year.

The cattle mart is a low building tucked away behind the town in the solemn shelter of the church and graveyard. The wind cuts over the bare remains of the old fair green, whistling through the corrugated-iron roof and empty cattle pens. Lorries, tractors and vans appear out of the grim morning, rumbling across the gravel forecourt. Small men sink deeper into big overcoats and tighten down well-worn caps as the wind whips along the first, sharp pellets of hail. Drivers climb down from lorry cabs:

"Hardy weather."

"You wouldn't put a ladder out this morning."

After a cold start on the bare hill-farms the farmers in Volkswagen Beetles begin to appear. Crawling down the street, hunched and half-awake and hanging out of the steering wheel, they squint and scowl at the day ahead.

The morning advances, and a thin winter light slants over rooftops pebbled with hailstones. Smoking chimneys show signs of life. Street doors open to reluctant dogs and schoolchildren rubbing eyes crusted with sleep. The pavements echo with the footsteps of sniffling scholars, bent with the cold and a burden of satchels.

The tractors and trucks form a ragged line in the mart yard by the unloading chute. Tail-gates come down and the animals rush blindly into a narrow cattle-crush to join an ordered single file, their brute strength contained by unyielding steel bars. A lock of hair is clipped from each broad back, a gob of paste goes on and a sticker with a number is slapped in place. The drovers collect cattle identity cards as you enter: export certificates a welcome bonus.

I surrender my animal, my card and export cert and make a note of my number for when the selling time comes around. The big-eyed cattle are herded along in the pens, bewildered by capture. All around, prized animals and proud owners are being separated. It is difficult to tell the animals apart now, as they are swallowed up amongst a score of similar shorthorns, black-pollys, Friesians, Limousins, Charolais and all the host of breeds in between.

In trots a mangy redhead. A poor cow, reared on rushes and louse powder; all skin and bones, a shabby coat, a long face and a broken heel. She is sent to the isolation pen for the day. Forlorn, forgotten and jeered at by better-fed farmers.

"Where did they find her?"

"Down from the far mountain, I'll gamble."

"Where the snipes wear wellingtons."

Inside, only one sales ring is in use today. Even the cattle seem subdued. At a busy mart, when you first plunge into the hot, reeking air, the uproar can be deafening. From a tubular steel maze of cattle pens and crushes packed with bellowing animals the steam rises from beefy flanks, wet snouts and the slippery, unwholesome floor. There are sudden roars from the booming bottoms of big-lunged bullocks that rattle the corrugated-iron roof and loosen the teeth in the mouths of old and yawning farmers.

Through the hot, sticky air, full of the smell of cattle and commerce and tobacco smoke, move the brown-coated cattle drovers and traders. And mixed amongst them are the shifty buyers, dealers and jobbers, asking devious questions and getting devious answers. And nobody giving anything away.

"What did you get for the heifer you sold before Christmas?"

"Ah! I got nothing for her. What did you get for yours?"

"I got half-nothing."

The men shout orders and discuss the prices and are here to do business. There is one face that appears every mart day. A man with the tops of his wellington boots turned down, his greatcoat tied about the middle with a hand-spun rope of hay. Ready for a day spent clambering over crowded cattle pens; tugging furry lugs, pinching the flesh of well-fed heifers, hankering after a slap along beefy haunches, that means more to him than a holiday by the sea.

"You wouldn't meet a finer animal in a day's walk," he declares, pulling at a wicked bullock's tail, delighting in the antics of maddened animals.

The business at the loading pens wears on long after midday. Then the crowd begins to gather around the sales ring. Over all the noise and steam and smoke comes the voice of the auctioneer. The real business of the day is about to begin. In a tight circle with a sawdust floor, the animals do a reluctant turn for the buyers. A bucking black-white-head gets a smart smack of the stick and shows a none-too-clean pair of heels on its trot around the ring. A haughty Continental Charolais, with garlic and molasses on its breath, does a lazy circle for the buyers and then lifts its tail before leaving the ring, unimpressed.

The buyers hang on the side of the ring like drowning men clinging to the edge of a raft. Shoulder to shoulder and cool as poker players they scrutinise every animal. Their trade is a miracle of co-ordination: eyes fixed on the chosen animal, ears tuned to make sense of the machine-gun rattle of the auctioneer. Their hands waving and signalling prices and bids with pointed fingers, open fists, raised eyebrows and a Masonic handshake for good measure. Orchestrated bids coming from the pit to the auctioneer conducting business from the podium. To be a good buyer you need an eye for a fine animal, a nose for a bargain, a thirst for a killing and a sixth sense no school or university can teach.

Above the ring on the wooden steps, big enough to double as bench seats and made to measure for the long strides of mountainy men, stand tight rows of sturdy and critical onlookers. With a dangling Sweet Afton, a bent pipe or the smouldering butt-end of a Woodbine gummed to a lower lip, this grim-faced jury watch the weights and prices. The business of the day is chewed over and, this being the New Year, often with the resolute sucking of a mint.

It would be fine to be a spectator today, but I have an animal to sell. I stand above the ring waiting for any animal that might pass for my own. Then I listen close to the bidding, measuring the selling price against my expectations. The neighbours at my back mutter oaths and sigh their discontent, chewing down the ends of their blackthorn sticks waiting for the outcome. When it is all done they pronounce that it was an unfair contest. The buyers had it all their own way. The seller was robbed.

"It's a disgrace. I don't know what sort of job you'd need to keep a farm going today."

I nod and fix a price in my head and swear I'll not sell for less.

After a long day standing around the ring the cold and the hunger creep in; through felt hats and flat caps, through mufflers and duffel coats, flannel shirts, long-Johns, and trousers the size of collapsed tents; through jackets burst at the shoulders, patched at the elbows but torn again at the sleeves; through greatcoats tied with string and anoraks with the quilted stuffing hanging out, the cold comes creeping deep into the brittle marrowbones and frozen hearts of bachelors without breakfasts.

It is time to retreat to the mart canteen. To the clatter of plates, the ring of forks and scraping knives. To the bubbling of hot soup and jolly women. To a steamy, hot, stew-smelling atmosphere where motherly women serve plates heaped with marbled and tender beef, mountains of mashed potato, crusty brown or white bread, with butter, buns and a portion of Swiss roll.

Sitting about the Formica-topped tables men stiff and silent with the cold rub calloused hands before wrapping them around scalding hot mugs of tea, or settling down to the tastiest, most welcome dinner of the week. In such a place a woman can lead a hungry miser into temptation.

"Go on, be a devil, and have some desert as well," the busty blonde teases, bending close to a willing ear.

A broken man, he fingers a rusty clasp, pokes and searches his old leather purse, and surrenders his savings to this sweet-talking Eve, offering a bite of sinfully sweet, hot and spicy apple tart.

Back at the sales ring it is time for me to take up position amongst the tense and anxious faces beside the auctioneer. My number comes a little closer with every turn of his slate. Each time he dusts off a number and chalks up a new weight in kilos, my day advances by another digit to that critical moment when I will have to sell.

It has been a long day since we first loaded the animals, clattering and scraping up the slippery tailboard of the truck under a hail of oaths and threats from a length of black plastic piping. Several hours have dragged by since I followed the slow procession of tractor trailers into town.

With time to kill I have walked past the trucks selling young calves in the depths of fodder-rationed and hungry January. Past vans with the back doors open displaying oilskins and donkey jackets, wellington boots and worm-doses, paraffin lamps, spades and spraying machines, rat-traps and candlesticks. The last reminders of the old street fairs.

The days of the horse trading between farmers, the spitting and the hand-slapping, the luck-money and the practised intervention of onlookers are gone. The dealers want only well-fed and finished animals. The order of the day is for lean beef for Continental tables. Casual banter remains but the talk hinges on the latest round of EC levies, subsidies, supplements and penalties. The only thing that counts now is that big clock-face above the mart ring that speaks in kilos. The common language of the Common Market.

The town trade slumped when the street fairs died. In the mart no money changes hands and deals will finish a week later with a cheque in the post.

In the old days wads of money were exchanged. And the farmers' wives came into town. A posse of head-scarfed women riding in on a rivet-rattling rural bus with a chesty diesel engine. They brandished long shopping lists; raiding drapers for woollen blankets and candy-striped flannelette sheets. They demanded winter duffel coats and sensible shoes for school-going children. It was a day for settling bills, buying treats and bringing home chirping boxes of day-old chickens. And the straw and leatherette shopping bags bulged towards bursting again. With the dealing done and the cattle tethered on the green the men crowded the bars and butcher shops, and never left town without a parcel of meat.

It is all so impersonal today. On a small farm like ours the animals are as well-known as the children. Though the cattle are there to make money the woman of the house has petted and coaxed them along since they were small calves. She has bucket-fed and suckled them with her fingers. She has weaned and foddered them with hand-picked best armfuls of hay. She has cleaned their barns and made their beds with dry straw. In the evenings she has walked the fields to bring her strays home before night. She has nursed them through runny noses, sore eyes, scours and coughs, talked to them.

"Suck ... suck ... suck. Poor little fella. Is your drink too hot? There's a good boy. I've picked a nice bit of hay for you. You'll eat that, won't you? Now, don't turn up your nose at me."

She has yelled at them, cursed and forgiven them: for tramping her clothes off the line, for breaking into her garden and eating the early cabbage plants, or biting the tops off spring flowers. She has fussed over buckets and tested the temperature of their milk as often as three times a day. She has plugged draughty holes in dry-stone barns and blocked up windows with rags and hay on the severest winter nights. She has wrapped the youngest and weakest, most spindle-legged new calves in blankets of wool when pneumonia threatened, and reared them until they were strong, thriving cattle running home with a dog at their heels.

My number is next on the slate. I hurry to the walled-off space behind the auctioneer where an animal that has been worried over for so long will be disposed of in a matter of minutes. The ordeal begins the moment the animal troops across the weighbridge and the long arm of the clock reaches after those precious extra kilos.

"What am I bid now for this fine animal? Who'll start the bidding at four hundred? Three fifty? Three hundred? Don't insult the man. Who'll give me three hundred?"

The auctioneer goes on demanding money and I stare at the floor until the starting price is settled.

It is a foreign language spoken by bidders and auctioneers all over the world: frenzied and distorted through ancient, dusty loudspeakers and rusty-voiced microphones. Meaningless to some, it is music to my ears. A melody of rising prices; of ever-increasing bids and still holding out for more. My body is rigid with tension, but I have seen connoisseurs of the cattle bidding trade lean grandly across these same hard cement steps, as comfortable as any Cleopatra on a feather divan.

"Keep her going, keep her going," says the voice inside my head.

The auctioneer turns and calls over his shoulder: "Do you want to keep us here all day?"

I shout back: "No sale."

Finally, after coaxing blood, sweat and tears from the stony-hearted buyers, after a dozen exasperated looks from the long-suffering auctioneer, after stubborn silences and pleas for one last bid, after all life seems finished around the ring, I give the nod.

"On the market."

The tongue-trotting is over and it is a final gallop to the finishing price. My animal is transformed: the flatfooted bullock of the morning becomes a Grand National favourite with my last penny riding on his back. In the final seconds the visions of all that hard work, all the effort to get this far, cloud the brain. The auctioneer's voice means nothing now. It might as well be a loose lid rattling on a boiling saucepan or a small dog furiously chewing butterscotch.

The bidders are exhausted at the last. It is a slow-motion finish as the auctioneer coaxes one final effort. There is a loud crack, as sharp and final as the fall of a guillotine blade, and the gavel comes down.

"Sold."

The auctioneer turns to me and says:

"It's a legacy you're getting at that price."

I step down, exhausted. Beneath the big coat I'm as limp as the auctioneer's thin paper docket in my hand with the sale price written in black and white. I got a good price and perhaps, but only perhaps, the others at home will be happy and not tell me I should have held out for more.

Outside, the dealers are loading their purchase. They will slip out of town the back way as soon as they finish in the mart office, on their night drive back to the docks and factories. I take a short-cut across the old fair green. The town is quiet again: a shop-girl mopping floors, a barman chatting to a customer, and dusk falling on the old fair green.

# OUT WITH IT

IN A THREE-ROOMED SCHOOLHOUSE at the top of the valley the blue Bangor slate roof shines after an April shower of hailstones. Sunlight strikes the long glass panes of the timber windows that slide down from the top on lead-weighted sashes. Seagulls swoop down into the school yard in search of bread crusts. The hailstones are slow to dissolve inside the perishing open-fronted outdoor shelter with the long plank seat. A cement-walled girls' toilet stands at one end of the shelter, and at the other end there is a rough and reeking boys' toilet where pissing contests go on.

In the lower classroom, wearing a home-sewn pinafore and dowdy shoes Mary Kate is up in front of the teacher for talking out of turn. Her gruff voice and farm ways are better suited to bucket-feeding a suck-calf with two fingers dipped into the warm milk while holding the head down for the calf to snuffling up its drink, than at keeping her nibs safe, or the blue ink smudges out of her copy book.

Miss Lynch stands by the coal-burning stove where the teacher's pets are allowed to keep their bottles of tea warm. Pale looking school pals sitting in twos at ink-well-fitted and pencil-grooved desks face the blackboard in their usual state of terror, while older girls recite their nine-times tables for the headmaster in the next room.

Using a sally rod cut from the roadside hedge Miss Lynch directs Mary Kate to hold out her hand. Silence. Then the air whistles with the speed of the first slap. A little red-welted hand drops, and the stick signals for the second hand to be raised. Another fast, stinging stroke, and through the swish and cut of the air Kate says to her teacher as if dealing with a kicking cow: "Aisy, ya bitch ya."

# A HARD SLOG

SKULLING CATTLE IS A ROTTEN and unnecessary job. Rotten because it leaves the person who has to take the horns off mature cattle feeling as shocked, demoralised and pained as the animals involved. And unnecessary because a dab of caustic soda when the horns were only the size of pimples under the fine hair on the skulls of the young calves would have burned the budding horns off at the root and spared me, the vet and their owner this barbaric ordeal.

But the cattle belong to 'the Brigadier' Duignan. And when it comes to farming the Brigadier is what you might call a *thougherer*: a great word for a farmer with no set or system on the place so that small jobs pile up into one big messy uphill slog. Further to the south of Ireland I heard the same kind of farming described as *mullocking*. And straight away you can picture the falling down barns and guttery gaps and farm fields ploughed up from overstocking into a muddy oxtail soup.

The Brigadier's real name was Tommy Paddy Andy. But years before, during a summer stint in the FCA, or the Free Clothes Association as these rag-tag army reserves billeted in Finner Camp near Ballyshannon were more fondly known, Tommy and the new recruits were out on the firing range with a Sergeant. There was a set of targets marked with coloured flags lined up along a bunker. The Sergeant told Tommy his was the green flag. Tommy took the Sergeant at his word and fired at the flag not the target and sent a bullet whistling by the Sergeant's ear and out over the firing rang past a lookout post.

After that he was given a broom handle instead of a rifle with the other ranks joking that by the time he left the FCA he had woodworm in his shoulder.

Back on the farm, when the jobs got the better of him the Brigadier went on the beer; leaving him even more work to face into when he sobered up. The hungry cattle would have strayed and fallen into drains trying to find ivy to eat.

There's a *mí-ádh* on that man, my mother would say: meaning the Brigadier was a conduit for misfortune. And I remember being sent by my father to the pub to find the Brigadier and tell him the storm had knocked over several of his haycocks.

Instead of taking action the Brigadier bought me a mineral and said, "When we finish our drinks we'll go out and chastise the wind."

Another time I had to find the Brigadier in the pub to tell him his cattle had broken into the good meadow and were tramping the hay he'd saved into the ground."

"They'll be sorry next winter," he said.

When he wasn't in the pub the Brigadier was one of these awkward men who always called to your house at an awkward hour looking for help with an awkward job in an awkward spot. And that's how I came to be lending a hand, a college student at the time, wrestling with the nose tongs to restrain the anaesthetized head of each brindled cow in the crush while the vet hacked through bone-textured horn.

As each horn came off gouts of blood spurted from the wound before the vet could tie the blood vessel, with the Brigadier following up the procedure with a sprinkling of purple-black disinfectant powder on the lividly exposed wound. And as we worked we kept tripping over the Brigadier's dog, 'Beauty', who took every freshly fallen horn in her mouth and ran off with it as soon as it landed in the mud.

Stomach churning doesn't' event start to describe the experience, so that when we had the job done and the cattle were let loose they stood on the spot shaking their heads and making low moans of distress.

"Throw them a loc of hay and they'll be grand," said the Brigadier, turning for the house.

When I had the cattle foddered, I broke a private agreement with myself never to drink strong spirits in the daylight hours, and I was glad of the glass of whiskey the Brigadier offered to me in his kitchen. We sat at opposite ends of the kitchen table where he kept all his needs within easy reach; the sliced pan of white bread, the open milk carton, the bag of sugar, the box of teabags, the pot of jam and the bottle of Milk of Magnesia. The only thing neat in the Brigadier's kitchen was the whiskey.

The postman arrived and dropped a letter in through the gap in the open sash window. It hit the floor with a good solid slap. Beauty the dog ran and fetched the letter in her mouth and brought it to her owner.

It looked like a luxury Christmas card and I wondered who might be sending the Brigadier Christmas greetings. The Christmas cards had dried up a long time ago since all the Brigadier ever did was sit in a kitchen chair opening envelopes and taking out whatever gifts of money came in the cards and while putting the money straight into his pocket tossing the cards themselves straight into the fire.

This was an unusually large, high quality envelope stamped with the name of an American law firm. Although addressed to the Brigadier in person he said he didn't know where he'd put his eyeglasses and he told me to, "Open it."

I sliced open the edge of the good envelope with the cleanest knife I could find on the table and unfolded a two-page letter on plush headed paper. I read the first paragraph and then stopped.

"It's a legacy," I said. "But the amount is your business." And I handed back the letter.

For the next couple of months I was away in college, but whenever I came home with the usual empty stomach and bag full of dirty laundry I heard the Brigadier's story in pieces. It began with the information that the Brigadier had a Granduncle and a Grandaunt on his late mother's side of the family in America. The Granduncle had died and having passed the bulk of his fortune on to his beloved wife there was still a lump-sum left over for his only living Irish relation. Namely, the Brigadier.

A week after he got hold of the legacy the Brigadier sold the hornless and hungry brindle cattle off the farm and replaced them with Charolais calves in prime condition. A month later the Brigadier sold the calves at a loss while on a drinking binge. A brand new tractor arrived on the farm but the Brigadier made ribbons out of the gearbox and the broken down tractor was left standing in the yard so long a blackbird finally built its nest inside the driver's cab.

Along with the tractor the Brigadier went through several new cars. He'd drive to the pub, crash on the way home and then abandon the wreck, taking the front and back number plates with him so passers-by wouldn't find out straight away he was after making a heap out of another new car.

Throughout this time there were parties in his house at all hours of the day and night to entertain the crowd of spongers he'd fall in with. And the Brigadier was known to throw out into the back yard the dirty plates and cups as soon as they were used, ordering more clean crockery from the local hardware whenever he ran out. You rarely saw him without a woman on his arm and none of them had scruples about helping the Brigadier make tatters out of the legacy.

Then one Saturday morning when I was back from college and driving into town I spotted the Brigadier walking. I pulled up to offer him a lift.

"Have you no transport?" I asked when he got in.

"The car is in the field below Stanton's Brae."

"What happened?"

"A combination of Guinness and loose gravel," he said, and I dropped him off outside Saddler's bar. Later when I went out to meet friends, the Brigadier was still there. He lifted his head when he saw me coming in and said, "Look at me now."

"What's wrong?"

"I'm the whole day on me own on the high stool."

"I'll get you a pint."

"I'll have a brandy," he said. "The hands are worn off me drinking pints."

The hard living had taken its toll on the Brigadier and even in the dimly lit front bar he was a shook looking outfit. I asked him if he needed a doctor. He shook his head and moved to the long seat under the window where he fell asleep. Seeing him stretched along the seat under the window one of the lads said, 'That's the busiest man in this parish - every time you see him he's flat out'.

At closing time I went to rouse the Brigadier and asked, "How are you getting home?"

He looked at me blearily and said, "By road, I hope."

As I helped him towards the front door he told me the legacy was gone.

"You enjoyed it while you had it," I said privately dismayed at the amount of money he'd squandered.

He gave me a crooked smile and stopped in the front porch. Bending down towards a wicker basket on the floor he caught hold of the pub owner's new dog still only a few months old. Picking up the Springer Spaniel puppy by the scruff of the neck he said, "You'll be a big dog before I'm back here."

The next time I enquired about the Brigadier's whereabouts I was told he was doing the month of November off the drink. Often the boys around home will come into the pub and order a pint of Smithwicks and a Hamlet cigar saying they're off the drink and the cigarettes for Lent. But the Brigadier went fully teetotal, living on strong tea and ham sandwiches.

I called in to see how he was getting on and he shoved up the groceries on the table to make a space for me. He would be a bachelor now until the end of his days though years before he had gone to see a widow woman with a view to a match being made. The Brigadier knew the same woman also had three good meadows and a big pasture field that sloped down into boggy ground where it met the River Shannon. The widow woman had more sense than to have anything to do with the Brigadier when she saw the cut of him; and when himself was asked what he thought of her he said she was "a nice woman with three fine meadows and a rough bottom".

We sat drinking mugs of tea and then the postman dropped in a letter through the open sash window. Beauty the dog ran to fetch the letter as soon as it hit the floor. Straightaway I recognised the firm of solicitors, and reckoned the Great-aunt in America must be dead.

Passing me the letter unopened the Brigadier said, "Burn it."

"It looks like another legacy?" I said.

But the Brigadier ordered me to toss the letter into the fire. Maybe he knew the letter wasn't really about more money coming to him and he was getting a rise out of me. At any rate, as the letter went in smoke up the chimney he turned to me and said, "I couldn't go through that again."

# HALLOWEEN

A YELLOW-BEAKED BLACKBIRD TRUMPETS the dusk as I take a walk by myself. I am twenty years old, single and feeling the frustration of living at home without a job with my parents on a hill farm in Arigna. After the bog lane, a sheep-path through a pasture field leads to a stone cabin built into the side of the mountain. The cabin roof is missing but the lintel stone over the door is still in place.

I recognise this as the homestead of a family at the bottom of the old social order of landlord, land agent and rent paying tenant. I stand a moment inside the ruin as the mountain fog dreeps down the stone walls. Then, I feel a presence, like the breath of a stranger on the back of my neck. And what overtakes me is not fear but a profound sympathy with the emotions in this household on bygone Halloween nights at the onset of another winter.

While I may be feeling hemmed in and powerless, any young woman growing up here would have had an even bleaker and uncertain future. She possessed few rights, no means of inheritance, and no standing in her society unless she got married. And one of the most immediate ways out of her predicament was to meet the right partner.

So in the springtime, when she blows the fluffy seed heads from dandelion 'clocks' in a single breath to make her wish come true, or in high summer when she plucks 'he-loves-me, he-loves-me-not' petals from the dog daisies crowning the ditches, or in the autumn when she twists a crab apple stem, and rhymes off the alphabet until the stem breaks on the first letter of the name of the lover yet to appear she has good reason for believing her whole future depends on it.

At the change in every season she naturally employs what is nearest to hand to solve the deepest problems of her heart.

And at Halloween especially she has a world-full of rhymes and rituals to try. There is the salted herring eaten at bedtime to make her thirsty, so that the man in her dreams who offers her a glass of water will be the one to marry her. With luck, she will not only see his face, she will see the quality of his clothes and the tools of his trade to guess at his station in life.

There is no foreknowledge of political correctness. And though she may soon marry if she chances on the ring hidden in the slice of brack she eats tonight, other slices hide a dried pea, a rag and a stick predicting the finder will end up either a spinster, a pauper or suffer beatings from their partner.

Perhaps it would be better to risk taking a broom out of the house to sweep around the stack of oats three times at midnight for an apparition with the face of her future husband to appear or a voice in the dark to speak his name.

But what if the Devil is waiting to trip her up? She could choke on a fish-bone in that salted herring. Or instead of a lover with a glass of water, she might see a coffin, foretelling death not marriage. Or as she circles that stack for the third time, in place of a vision of her future husband, she will be confronted by an evil spirit so terrifying her hair will turn white overnight.

Lifetimes separate us, and I wasn't there so I don't know what finally led to this cabin being abandoned, but my own circumstances have made me appreciate the attraction of any trick to discover your destiny.

And later on that same Halloween night, I find myself standing amongst young nieces and nephews making a game out of hand-me-down Halloween superstitions. Their interest is prompted by a sense of fun not desperation.

Yet I can't help feeling nervous at the thought that some part of my future is being determined as I stand blindfolded while they shuffle a row of saucers on the kitchen table. One holds a ring representing marriage, another holds coins for wealth. There is clay for sickness or death in another saucer that I hope to avoid. And as it happens, when I reach out my hand I touch the saucer full of water, which predicts that if I am to find love and fulfilment I have a journey ahead of me.

# DEPARTURES

OUTSIDE THE AIR-CONDITIONED TERMINAL at John F. Kennedy Airport it is a sweltering 90 degrees Fahrenheit. The air is high with aviation fuel. Sweat trickles down the back of a uniformed baggage-handler called Lou who is filling in for me. I have shed my airport staff I.D.s to become another statistic in the never-ending business of departures and arrivals.

We ride the Atlantic jet-stream to Shannon in five hours. Then I pick up a rented car to take me back to the townland where I was born. It is late summer over here. The skies are grey; a white-cap of mist on the far mountain; rain in the wind; a lonesome wind in the big trees and the stormy hedgerows. And that radiance in the west, as I come around a bend in the lane into the low evening light. I had forgotten this emptiness.

The home place at the end of the lane is a slumbering vault now, rain-downs on the once white walls. The garden is a thistle-patch, the sulphur smell of nettles about the weathered stone. The cottage rose, pink lupin and dahlia beds are all gone. Only the briars and the stinging nettles took permanent root here.

I catch a bar of laughter coming across the fields. Children from the new bungalows have come out to cycle rings around the road on a shared bicycle. The younger ones take turns holding a terrier pup, wet and wriggling between bare arms, a long tongue licking ticklish ears. Boys with bicycles and wellington boots, sniffles and gap-teeth. Mirrors of my own youth, reared out of doors amongst the hawthorns and hiding places up sycamore and elm trees. Yes, I know the pattern of their hedge retreats intimately. My childhood, too, is fenced about these fields.

They watch me. The boy from the Bronx, returned to sell his past. The roadside fields of a small family farm, broken into lots and sold for sites for bungalows on the hill. New homes for neighbours' daughters, schoolgirls in my time, grown to young wives in curves of motherhood.

I have the dust of grey asphalt streets and the dusty brown ball-parks of America in my pockets. I had forgotten the natural green of this farmland: green of trees and green of hedgerows, green of meadows and pasture, green of gaps and shadows. But I remember a dancing cloud of midges caught in the last, slanting shaft of evening sunlight, the call of blackbirds in the late dusk, the damp air of enclosed paths, ticklish and threaded with wandering spider-webs. Moths on the wing at dusk in poor fields dripping with rain-water pearls.

The whole property is falling down before the forces of neglect and natural decay. I find Dutch elm disease ravaging the limbs of the old elm trees around the house, the bolts and nails of tree-houses buried deep in their seasonal rings that compass my growing years.

I take up a handful of wet grass for the earth-smell of it, and remember the very first time I heard of the city of New York and the Empire State Building. "The eighth wonder of the world," my father said, holding my small hand, walking home through the rough pasture behind a black and white milking cow.

Going around the back of the house now, past the fallen down cow-barns and roofless sheds, I take the path to the drinking well. And pushing through each summer's new growth of unchecked bindweed and ivy, I find a trickle of country lore coming back to me. Names of plants and wild flowers not seen since I left for America: fairyfingers, ox-eye daisy, saxifrage, heart's-ease, and forget-me-not.

And I recall running in from the next meadow field, rich with the smell of seasoned hay under the sun, to bring a bottle to this same spring well. Plunging clear glass into clearer water, while the bottle bubbled and sucked up stone-cold water where it came clean out of the earth between dancing pebbles. Then running back hard in plastic sandals to bring a drink to my father. A tidy build of a man in a white shirt with the sleeves rolled up, working in a mountain meadow field long ago.

A man alive to the smell of new-mown hay on the breeze, or the horror of frogs caught on the rattling blade of the mowing machine, as the saw-teeth levelled the regular swards of June hay. Then taking out the back-sward with rakes together, working our separate ways around the border of the field.

I miss that purest satisfaction: of a clean, pale-stubbled field, with long shadows reaching out from the haycocks and hedgerows as the sun dipped behind the hills. A veil of mist rising over the still river. The far mountain, pink in the last of the light. A summer moon, low on the horizon, for that last round-up after a day of gathering, building, heading and roping the haycocks. Man and boy, working in a simpler world to an understood rhythm.

I was my own master then, picking up discarded hay-forks, waterbottles and cast-off jumpers. Closing the gaps and leaving the field at nightfall. Taking a strange pride in being the last one out.

On my way out now I find myself standing under the old sycamore tree at the road gate. I hear the drone of late-working bees amongst the mottled leaves. Seed-pods helicopter down.

I loved it best standing here in winter, late in the frosty night, when the stars glimmered more fiercely through the hard, bare branches. Had I somehow foreseen constellations of car headlights streaming along the Franklin D. Roosevelt elevated highway? Standing at the half-way point along the boardwalk across the Brooklyn Bridge, looking through the network of steel cables at the amber and white-lit windows of Manhattan. The floodlit crown of the Empire State Building sending shafts of red, white and blue light into a vaulted heaven. Under my feet, the ceaseless vibration of traffic, and the fretwork of these East River bridges humming the headlong song of America.

The country air comes thick with fragrant and invisible pollen. The very breath of summer. I bend towards a thicket of evening-perfumed honeysuckle. That smell, the utter quiet, the solitude, raise a familiar shiver on my back, and memories of those first, half-formed longings for travel.

I stop again where the mountain road dips towards the spangled lights of the village to study a derelict property under lonesome dales. I would not dare press my face to its clouded windows in this falling dusk. It is the home of a ghost. The ghost of a retired labourer, who told me once that in his youth he, too, had been "one of the boys from the Bronx".

When his legs could carry him about these country by-ways no more, my family had found him this place to live, a basic shelter from the elements on the side of a mountain. A quiet, empty place, where memories of his days labouring in the humid glare of the building sites of America mingled freely in his imagination with the farming traditions of his youth. On a winter's evening by a fire of turf stolen from the mountain he would confide in me:

"I heard them last night, Sir. A *meitheal* in Barney Kiernan's field. All night they were talking and shouting, and I heard their shovels striking stones in them hungry ridges."

And then he would describe for me the gangs of shirtless men in cloth caps and heavy boots breaking open the heart of the Manhattan bedrock for the waves of glimmering new skyscrapers rising against the sun-white heavens. The rush of strange people and machines amongst the geometric order of grid-iron city streets. Meetings with coloured men, Chinamen wearing ponytails, Polish men, Jews and Italians. The foreign tongues and foreign ways of life down in the siren-loud canyons of Manhattan by day, and the yellow-brick tenements of the Bronx by night.

He quit America and came here, to spend the last years of his life in a strange no man's land, lost between Old and New Worlds. I was a child then, rooted in a small-farm world. And I lived in awe of his hobo life, his freedom from family chores, schoolbells and bedtimes. When he came calling to our house I hid behind the barns and watched him steal an egg for his supper, or a few potatoes or vegetables out of the garden. He never took more than he needed, and we knew that for him the stolen bite tasted sweeter than charity.

Later I would go to his mountain shack and sit watching the old boy from the Bronx drink his tea coloured with clotted milk from long-standing bottles in the windows. And he would spit on a black, iron frying-pan to see if it was hot enough to sizzle his fat, bristled ends of bacon and stolen onions. And then to bed, sleeping off his daily tonic of porter.

"The day I can't walk down that road for a bottle of stout, I'm done for, Sir," he told me.

Most nights, the old boy from the Bronx staggered back alone and dizzy, breaking the mountain silence with regular throat-clearing coughs. He tripped one time, and rolled from the roadside ditch into the field below. I happened to come along later and I heard a familiar voice call out of the darkness:

"Are you on the road, Sir?"

"I am."

"In that case, Sir, I'm off the mark."

I take the mountain road down to the edge of the village where the community centre stands. I earned my first wage packet there, building a wall in the women's toilet. The wall sagged in the middle, but I had taken the first step of a young apprentice off that family farm on the side of the mountain. I got the first taste of builder's lime in my mouth on that job, and the first corrosive cement blisters on my fingers. And a sense of the foundations of my future life being laid out for me.

From the roof, where I spent my time with my shirt off in the sun at lunch hour, whistling at the girls going by in summer cotton, I saw the first of my neighbours calling at the local barracks to get their passport application forms stamped. That trickle became a flow, and carried most of my emigrant generation away.

On the village street, now, I meet a survivor. One of the few small farmers left up there on that lonesome mountain. One of a dying breed of black-faced bachelors. That neglected and hidden country manhood, known by the shine in their old suits, the grime along rumpled and worn shirt collars and cuffs, the burnt-yellow nicotine-coloured fingers and nails and the yesterday shave. That telling black in the pores: the mark of men who no longer wash, no longer care, all hope of greater fulfilment grizzled and weathered away.

He could be the last inhabitant on the planet; a bachelor until he dies. For women are hard to come by, up there amongst the short grass, wet rocks and low rain-clouds. But he knows where he belongs. Stepping easy in a patchwork of old suits, flat cap down over his ears, his long coat belted about a thin frame, walking a narrow black bicycle for company.

Watching his even-paced progress in this empty street I find it hard to believe that in forty-eight hours from now I will be standing on the Grand Concourse at Fordham in the Bronx again, watching the evening traffic grinding through the smoke-hot dusk after a day of big summer heat. Then taking a downtown train under crowded Manhattan streets and crossing into Brooklyn, where it will be a muggy eighty-two degrees down on Montague Street. The neighbourhood streets will belong to strolling couples, newly arrived emigrants establishing a foothold, cinnamon-skinned youths loafing or jostling on the corners and the car fenders. And I will stop for a couple of chilled beers and shoot the breeze with a couple of buddies before going on to weekend work in the alien glare of this endless melting-pot city.

The old boy props his bicycle against a rusty petrol pump. We step over a sheepdog lying across the pub door and we go in together.

There are groceries at the top end of the bar counter, the bare essentials for drinking men: tins of corned beef, sardines in oil, loaves of bread and half-pounds of butter, and strong, untipped cigarettes. Bachelor's provisions.

After the brash and raucous bars of Brooklyn and the Bronx this is a den of empty shadows, silent men and old upholstery. The men consider their bottled stout and half-ones. Welcomes are muted as I settle into the curious comfort of my own kind.

I shout a drink for the old boy who came in with me. He takes a bottled beer and asks:

"What do you make of life over there in the States, anyway?"

And I tell him.

"Sometimes I think I've wandered off the mark.

# WHERE PEACE COMES DROPPING SLOW

IT WAS EARLY IN THE NEW TERM and I wasn't long back in college after spending another summer working in America. The leaves were just beginning to turn a glorious autumn-kindled gold, and I had this pent-up longing for open air and a day spent catching up with my own thoughts.

The wise adult knows how the things that made you happy as a child will make you happy as an adult, experienced in a more comprehensive and comprehended way. And I had never lost my love of solitary trips into the heart of nature.

So I hired a wooden boat at Riverside with the intention of rowing up the Garavouge – which must be amongst the shortest rivers in Ireland, flowing from Lough Gill through Sligo town out into the sea. Lough Gill though is a big lake, best visited in perfect weather, since it has a reputation for never surrendering all of its lost and drowned. And I was nervous and unaccustomed to rowing as I took the wobbling boat out awkwardly onto the river.

I soon managed not to splash too much water as I found a rhythm with the oars. And the morning light bounced off the peaceful water, while in bird's eye view the lake itself was a perfectly polished mirror reflecting Sliabh Daeane and Slish Wood. Or Sleuth Wood as Yeats calls it in *The Stolen Child*, where the highlands at Dooney Rock dip into the lake, and "the flapping herons wake the drowsy water rats".

Amongst the islands on Lough Gill, the most famous is the Lake Isle of Innisfree. But that island stood at the opposite end of the lake and was comparatively tiny, with barely enough room for nine bean rows or a hive for the honeybee. Handier by far, for an amateur oarsman, was Cottage, or Beezie's Island, named after Beezie

Gallagher who lived the life Yeats only ever dreamed of.

When her cattle-dealer husband died in 1934, Beezie continued to live as a hermit in her thatched cottage on the island, rowing into town to collect her pension on Fridays or whenever the weather permitted. Sadly, she lost her life in 1951, when sparks caught in the thatch on a stormy night causing her house to burn down.

And as I rounded Wolf Island, I found a ghostly memorial 'smoke' rising from the lake, caused in reality by the surface water being warmer than the overhanging frosty air. Although legend had it there was a secret city submerged under these same waters, once ruled over by the chieftains Omra and Romra buried under the twin stone monuments crowning the nearby Cairn's Hill. And these wispy vapours coiling around my boat might easily have been the smoke rising from underwater chimneys.

Poetry and legend were woven everywhere into this landscape. But I had to keep my mind on making every stroke of the oars count. And soon my confidence increased, and the boat began to glide smoothly along the glassy expanse of open water.

Then looking over my shoulder a bosky island appeared – bearing in on me it seemed, rather than my boat closing in on it.

At last the keel met gritty black sand. I hopped out and hauled my boat ashore, and felt like the first person every to lay claim to the place. Then wading through waist-deep ferns under the broadleaf canopy I reached a sunlit clearing, and stood transfixed by nature's perfect Zen garden balance of moss and rock and clustered rowan berry.

In America I'd worked alongside people on their second and even third heart bypass still unsuccessfully toiling to earn the kind of money needed to be able to afford to take a boat out onto open water where they lived and stop on an island as peaceful and lovely as this. It made me feel privileged and restored.

I soon came out on the other side of the island where I sat down on a grassy sward facing the far shore. It felt good to listen to the muffled drum-roll of far away traffic, and to be so happily unavailable.

By the time I started back, the sunlight was already turning pale pink and evening gold, and the countryside was barely visible in a deepening blue haze. I had come looking for the tonic of wildness and found it in fuchsia sweet and snowberry pure abundance. And when I tied up again at Riverside the light-drenched, airy and expansive joy of my day on the lake made me want to share the ordinary richness I'd found like an adventurer freshly returned from an undiscovered paradise.

# THE PROPOSAL

JOHNNY WAS A BACHELOR, a coal-miner and a small-time cattle dealer. He could be rough, uncouth and blunt, but he always spoke his mind. For a while he went out with a local girl called Mary Reynolds, and then he went to see her father to ask for the daughter's hand in marriage. The father didn't want Johnny next nor near his precious only daughter. And he turned down Johnny's proposal saying: "The man that marries my daughter will be decent, clean, honest, sober and hard-working and have land of his own and money in the bank."

"I understand," said Johnny. "You want her to do better than her mother."

# CHRISTMAS LIGHTS

MANY YEARS AGO we paid more than we intended for a good set of Christmas tree lights. They weren't especially fancy. But they turned out to be amazingly reliable. So as soon as we are done with the lights each year, we pack them away safely in their original box along with the other decorations, until the following Christmas when they are unpacked again with the bags of baubles, the strings of beads, the tinsel, the garlands and the Santa hats.

In more recent years we've added a new Christmas tree stand that can be topped up with water to stop the tree from shedding. Despite which, the floor and rug always ends up littered with pine needles. But we grew up with real trees and we wouldn't want an artificial job for all its handiness and durability.

With the tree in place, and before we can get decorating, the lights have to be tested. Each year we plug them in and cross our fingers and flick the switch. When the lights spring on, it feels like the magic of Christmas starting all over again.

Lit and looped around the tree on their braided green wire, the lights inspire a deeper sense of happiness in me, in fact, than the whole grandiose display of Christmas illuminations brightening the streets and shop windows of the town. Not that I object to the whole gaudy spectacle of Christmas in the 'High Street', even if there's reason to believe that the true spirit and meaning of the season is everywhere exploited, manipulated, and in bondage to commerce and inflated prices.

Even so, a soaring sweetness of feeling overflows in me at the touching splendour of the Christmastide illuminations, aglow in the marzipan December dusk, with a brass band playing and a choral group singing old-time carols, and collectors out gathering for charity against a church-steepled skyline; and spicy smells of cinnamon and cloves and zesty lemons wafting from the mince pies and mulled wine of the merrymakers greeting and gathering in popular cafes and bars, and the tearful homecomings and reunions too, at the airports being reported on the news.

This is the way Christmas presents itself to us nowadays. But what comes to mind for me, looking at our own string of lights is how each single bulb twinkles like a happy memory of an earlier Christmas to form a succession of memories that extends back years and decades.

And where the span of our Christmas lights finish, they link up in my imagination with those earlier rainbow-coloured paper garlands that we had when we were children, and which opened up like accordions and stretched from one corner of the kitchen ceiling to the other, complemented by school copybook flat decorations that opened astoundingly into paper bells.

Decorations as perennial in their day as the time-honoured garlands of ivy and the bunches of red-berried holly that people employed before readymade paper chains, and which connect us back even further in time to an era when a burning candle trimmed with holly shone in every window on the eve of Christmas in honour of the Holy Family and entire parishes – without the blessing of electric – were wondrously lit up like ocean liners.

The decorative trappings of Christmas link in too with old-time household rituals, where seasonal meals were prepared for the family involving three and sometimes five kinds of warm bread, that included treacle cakes, and potato cakes and griddle-bread baked on the open fire, traditionally eaten with poached salmon when everyone was finally home on Christmas Eve.

And because our fondest attachments to Christmas start in childhood, I love chatting to my seniors about their earliest memories of Christmas, and the ageless joy of waking up to find their stockings loaded with sweets and pasteboard fripperies, spinning tops and paper bugles with a reed in them that I'm told on Christmas Mornings, "You'd hear all across the whole townland."

Christmas is a Christian feast, of course. But it celebrates these human values too. The decorating and the cooking, the showing and the sharing, the looking back and the furthering, which like that set of lights spanning our tree each year, not only reaches around its pine boughs, but stretches reliably from year to year, and extends in harmonious succession the bright fond memories of Christmas celebrations shared by each generation with the next.

# TAKING OFF FOR CHRISTMAS

ON CHRISTMAS EVE, Emmet McLoughlin arrived back from England. He rolled off the ferry driving a Jaguar XJS. "The same car Margaret Thatcher used to drive," he boasted to the lads when he pulled up outside the pub.

In the front bar he swung the key-ring hung on his little finger for everyone to see and ordered drinks for the house. Then tugging a chunky wallet out of his back pocket to prove he was well-wedged with cash for the holiday, he flashed a glimpse of a pilot's ID.

"O yes, I have my hundred hours done," he bragged. "And did I tell you about the time I flew to the Canaries and the pilot offered me the controls if I wanted to take her in."

"Can you pay for the round of drinks first," said the bar-owner, "just in case this landing goes wrong."

Later, when Emmet headed for the men's toilet out the back – nicknamed the Tom Crean Suite on account of the polar conditions – the lads reckoned that Emmet's papers were out of a Christmas cracker, and the only flying solo he'd ever done was over the handlebars of a bicycle.

Night began to fall and there was a fine sprinkling of snowflakes. Enough to cause Emmet's friends to knock back their drinks, turn up their coat collars, and head for home.

Now you'd see a heavier dusting of caster sugar on top of a mince pie than the amount of snow on the ground, but in the car-park nothing would do Emmet only get out the snow chains kept in the boot of the Jag.

At the same time, a mile beyond the town Tom Packie, Emmet's neighbour, had taken refuge in his local pub after the wife Bridie shooed him out of her kitchen so that she could have everything ready for their Christmas dinner the next day. Walking home in the dark, Tom Packie was enjoying the sight of all the houses lit up across the countryside in honour of the Holy Family, when he heard an unholy racket coming up the road behind him.

In the frosty darkness he saw sparks flying and heard chains rattling and he threw himself up against the ditch, convinced that the Devil himself was coming. But it wasn't the Devil in his coach and four; it was Emmet's snow-chains biting into the snow-free tarmac road.

"What are you doing hiding behind the bushes?" Emmet shouted when he stopped and lowered the window. And having given Tom Packie a hop he treated him to a spin home in the jag.

Back at the house Emmet opened the bottle of duty free he had with him for Tom Packie to make hot-ones. "You don't need sugar or anything with this stuff," he said, "just a skite of hot water is all."

Tom Packie found that he liked the taste. And having warmed up with the first drink they made another round.

Then they started to get hungry.

Bridie had the table set and everything looking lovely. And though Tom Packie loved his turkey fresh out of the oven she always roasted it the night before. It sat cooling now on a big silver platter, golden and tantalising.

Emmet convinced Tom Packie to share a wing.

"A noble bird," said Tom Packie chewing happily.

"You could eat that without a word in your head," Emmet agreed. And seeing as a bird never flew on one wing, they ate the other wing between them and boiled the kettle again.

The juicy warm turkey only made them hungrier, so they had a leg apiece. And by the time they finished another couple of rounds their hands were reaching out without thinking to glaum wads of turkey meat off the breast.

It took until the day after Saint Stephen's for Bridie to show up at Emmet's front door. She had a Mass Card in her hand, the second one she said she got signed by the priest to have masses said over her husband who still wasn't able to crawl out of his sick bed. Next she told him that not alone had she no husband on Christmas Day, she had no turkey either when she came down in the morning and found a bare carcass and an empty bottle of Southern Comfort. And then on her way to Mass she found bits of broken snow-chain in the lane, a car stuck in the hedge, and a pilot's license lost on the ground.

# A SMALL REBELLION

AT THE END OF OCTOBER my father had come down with a cold. We had visits from the lady doctor. The fire was revved up in the kitchen to warm the room for an examination. My father dressed and came down from the bedroom and sat close to the hob. We listened for the car outside. I met the doctor on the front street and escorted her into the house. Then my mother closed the panel door and waited about doing small jobs in the scullery. The doctor was patient and kind. We all knew it was dangerous.

After a discreet absence my mother came back into the kitchen to set a tray with tea and biscuits for the doctor. She found my father and the doctor talking and smoking together. Out at the car, when the doctor had issued a prescription and was giving me a few tablets in a bottle for my father to be going on with she said: "You could try keeping him off the cigarettes, but it would add nothing to his life now. He won't change and you couldn't hope to give him more than a month. The withdrawal symptoms and the suffering involved would make his last days a misery for everybody, especially for your father."

I suppose he had been smoking since he was twelve or fourteen years old. Sweet Afton, with the Robert Burns poem printed on the box:

*Flow gently, Sweet Afton, among thy green braes,*
*Flow gently, I'll sing thee a song in thy praise.*

Or war-time Woodbines, sold singly or in the original blue packets. As a boy it was daring and forbidden to smoke while watching Hopalong Cassidy in the picture house, and as a young man in the fifties it was fashionable and without danger, even for all-action cowboys and matinee idols. Later, in the public bar, a pint wouldn't be the same without a cigarette. But there was a history of weak chests and asthma in the family: brothers and sisters had died young. Even so, he loved his cigarettes. Couldn't do without them.

"Would you ever run down to the shop for ten cigarettes and a box of matches," he'd say, just when we were all settled for the night, watching the television.

Then the song and dance would start.

"Could you not wait until the morning?" my mother would say.

"Give your lungs a rest. Can't you see the cigarettes are killing you?"

"I'll go myself," he'd say, going out into the hall and putting an arm into his coat.

"No, I'll go," I'd volunteer, knowing that if he went he would spend the rest of the evening in the pub.

He wasn't a late-night drinker, more a four o'clock until eight o'clock man. A bunty-tailed terrier followed him everywhere he went and always sat under his seat by the window in the front bar. He would meet the pitmen stopping off from work, and drink with them until the crowd started to come in. The young bloods called him "Scampeen". Part mockery and part affection. The talk ranged from pruning roses to the proper way to eat cream crackers with a priest's housekeeper over a good carpet.

Then he would ask one of the lads to leave him up the road. He would buy a round, and when they had finished their drink they would drop him at the road gate. He took his time on the lane. Stopping to bend in the middle, leaning his hands on his legs just above the knees, waiting to get his wind back. You could hear him coughing long into the dusk.

The terrier would grow restless and leave him then, rushing ahead to meet my mother in the yard, where she was getting the last of her jobs done in the failing light. She knew my father took blackouts when the colour of his face turned deep red and the coughing bouts deepened to a noiseless spasm. She couldn't sit easy in the house until she heard him coughing in the lane and she knew he was back again safe.

He wasn't long in the door before he went upstairs to bed, the clock radio turned up. When supper was ready my mother would call up to him:

"Are you coming down for a cup of tea."

"Bring it up."

"Bad luck to you, couldn't you do all that for a person?"

No answer. Just the sound of the radio. And she'd relent and say, "Do you want a bit of currant bread with it?"

"Aye," he'd answer quietly.

The real battle was to get him to cut back on the Woodbines, and then to get him to change over to filter-tipped cigarettes. In the beginning he would just break off the filters and smoke the remainder down to a damp end burning on his bottom lip, his jaws two stubborn hollows sucking the last drag of smoke out of the butt.

An American aunt posted us a set of six brown plastic filters of different lengths and strengths that were designed to lower Daddy's need for nicotine in stages. He used one of the shortest and weakest filters for a week or so, and then only when we were watching. After seven days of neglect in the bottom of his pocket, amongst the small coins and loose tobacco, it was in such a foul state we had to accept defeat.

The battle had been lost a long time before, but in the last months it was hard to take it when he started up his Ventolin nebuliser, a clear plastic mask over his nose and mouth, breathing in his medication in a compressed air spray to open the pores of his lungs. And the minute his lungs were ready to take in the oxygen he lit up another cigarette.

"I know the cigarettes are killing me," he'd say.

"It's psychiatric care you need," was all my mother could say in return.

He spent hours up in his bedroom reading short articles out of *Ireland's Own* magazine and listening to the clock radio. Sitting up in bed at the mention of the corn-crakes in "Pat Murphy's Meadows" in summers long ago. And he was very fond of Tommy O'Brien: an unlikely radio star who specialised in playing the opera greats from a private collection of crackling 78s. Other times you would find him in the sitting room, the air blue with smoke, watching Hurricane Higgins play snooker or Harvey Smith show jumping on the television in the middle of the day with the curtains closed.

"I'm going up for ten minutes of a rest," he would say when the house got busy around him, as we tried to hustle him out into the fresh air.

"I'm not in good fettle myself. I could lie down too," my mother would respond, "It's time I got a bit selfish."

"I wondered when it would start."

"You're only interested in that cigarette."

"I'm going back up to bed, to get away from your tongue."

"Go where you'll get care."

On a mild day my father might stand on the front street for a while, with both hands on the wall around the garden. He stood looking out towards the beehives and, following the line of his sight, I was reminded of a time when he would sit on his hunkers for hours watching the bees come and go on the ramp in front of the hive. He loved to watch the young worker bees warming their bodies for flight, and the returning bees dancing for the hive: selflessly directing the other worker bees to a rich pollen find. But I think it was the patience and the courage of each small worker bee that he admired most. Small, exhausted bees resting after arrival, bright loaded pollen sacks on either side of their tired insect bodies.

And even though his wind was gone he mustered his strength when a swarm of bees gathered in a clump in one of our apple trees with the queen bee lodged somewhere in the middle of the tight cluster.

"A swarm in May is worth a load of hay; a swarm in June is worth a silver spoon," he said.

It was late September now but he had me fetch a cardboard box and, without the protection of gloves or a veil, he lowered the buzzing clump of bees into the box and closed the lid. He had no fear he said because he knew the different high angry buzz a bee makes when he's upset and ready to sting, 'ready to die to protect the hive'. And he took care to explain to me that in the bees' world the old drones were regarded as a burden on the store of honey and were put out of the hive to die before the winter.

After the exertion he stood for a long time gasping for air, searching the autumn fields with his big, straining eyes, his thoughts concentrated on his breathing, trying to loosen the knotted lump of airways in his congested lungs

"They'll lift that phlegm in the hospital for you," my mother said to him, but we were on the brink of winter and we could see he had no interest.

"The women will be all right," he'd say, leaving my mother to do the shopping, and ducking into Austie Wynne's pub for a pint of stout as soon as he had been fitted for a new jacket ahead of the doctor's visit.

Daddy never wore a suit. He liked a sports jacket and a plain pants, a white shirt and tie. He wore a dap of Brylcream in his fair hair and liked to sport a badge in his lapel: a small gold rose or an Easter Rising commemorative paper lily held in place with a pin.

There were Sinn Féin dances in the Parish Hall, and organised bus journeys to the border to fill in the craters in the unapproved roads dynamited by the British Army that he avoided, though he had returned from England because he wasn't happy there.

As an active, outdoors man all his life he had felt his individual freedom restricted in London. So he mounted his own small rebellion. He raided a private lake and kept the brown trout he took alive in his bathtub until he could bring them in damp, rolled newspapers on the back of a friend's BSA motorbike to small lake in wooded public park where they planned to fish undisturbed in the years to come.

"You can't be a rebel all your life," my mother reminded him after this escapade. "If you're going to get on in this world you have to conform sometime."

"You couldn't put manners on Paddy," he answered, assuming his own obstinate nature to be a national virtue.

I could not say what his religious beliefs were. There was that golden rosary society badge in his lapel worn only for show, but he had made a curiously pagan vow years ago, that if he was left his teeth he would not shave on a Sunday. He had good teeth. And even though he took me and my brothers Sean and Owen to mass, when I started kicking up a fuss he left me to my own devices saying I was old enough to know my own mind.

He kept a well-thumbed Holy Bible by his bedside but curiosity, kindness and respect were the virtues he esteemed.

"If you haven't anything good to say, then you shouldn't bother opening your mouth."

On summer evenings after work he'd take a fibreglass rod with a spinning reel and walk down to the river to cast for a trout he had spotted rising near the bridge. He would light a cigarette and blow smoke to keep the midges away and tell me about the time he was out fishing on the lake when a fog came down. With no sign of the shore and nothing to navigate by, he was able to make it to dry land by watching the wake in the water behind the boat and keeping it straight.

Coarse fishing and rough shooting brought out the best in him. And on patient walks with me as a child he trained me to listen to the seed-pods of the wild broom bursting open in the summer heat. He taught me how to tell a rabbit from a hare, a red from a grey squirrel, and spot a kestrel drop fast on a young bird. Hedge-schooling me in the names of plants: the wild pea, also know as vetch, honeysuckle or the wild woodbine that gave off its perfume at night since it was pollinated by moths. Foxglove or fairy finger, also known as digitalis. Woodruff, dog daisy and eyebright.

"Daddy, you're a walking encyclopaedia," I said to him one time, and he was proud for both of us.

When I got older he took my younger brother Owen and me to a coppice and showed us how to build a 'hide' and camouflage our work with branches and ferns. Then we sat and waited like terrorists for the pigeon flocks coming in to roost on a windy evening. Passing his shotgun to me he helped me shoulder it properly to avoid the kick of the shot. Under his guidance I became an early riser trusted with his shotgun. And when I knew how to hunt on my own and make a professional kill, he took care to curb that power.

"Never, ever, point a gun at anyone, even if you think you know for definite the gun isn't loaded," he said. And whether I was handling a shotgun, tackling a new job, dealing with people or dealing with trouble I should keep in mind how "A little bit of manners goes a long way."

On another occasion he said I shouldn't be so "Obstreperous". For he delighted in new words; while I teased him telling him our neighbour said after the good summer he had a "Robundance" of hay this year.

Though he was a gardener by trade he rarely ate vegetables, yet he loved to experiment with new varieties. And when my older brother took an interest in electronics Daddy found him a book called *The Junior Electrician*, which showed how to make electromagnets from a nail and coiled copper wire, and a crude microphone from the carbon bars found in old flash-lamp batteries. When Sean got a bit older my father loaded up an ass and cart with old valve radios and crystal sets left behind in a shed by a German refugee called Brock, who had made his living fixing radios and charging wet batteries during the war.

Soon everybody was getting tangled in Sean's experimental telephone wires and transmitter systems. And when my mother gave out about the danger Daddy said in his defence: "He has great brains."

When I started to make model heads out of the blue daub from the ditches and found the smooth stoneware clay could be baked in the oven and then painted with acrylics I created a horde of monsters inspired by the special effects of Ray Harryhausen. "Express yourself," my father said and let me follow my designs into art school.

Now the doctor had warned us we were running out of time with him. But he had been in bad health for so long. The same doctor had said last year we would be lucky if we had him for the Christmas. He had been anointed then. And here he was, a year later, listening to the radio and coughing and smoking on the quiet, no matter how much we pleaded with him.

It was the start of November and I was living at home again helping my mother to look after him. He needed help now climbing the stairs but he liked to pass the evening by the fire in the sitting room. Afterwards we helped him up the stairs and settled him into bed.

It must have been about two o'clock in the morning and I was still up when I heard him come back down the stairs. This was unusual.

"I'm seeing things in my head," he said. "I don't know what's wrong."

"It's just the tablets making him dopey," my mother said. "He'll be all right when he lies down."

I led him back to bed. But he wouldn't lie down. I had to raise him up and stack the pillows behind his back. There was a smell of Brylcream and sweat and tobacco from his nightwear. I came back later and he appeared to be dozing. His breathing sounded better and I laid him back in the bed. I was about to leave the room when he woke up. He wanted to be propped up again. I thought he was being awkward: if he just lay down quietly he would soon drop off and get a good night's sleep. But I came back and propped him up with extra pillows so he could sleep sitting up. I guessed he would light a cigarette the minute I left the room.

I looked in one more time before going to bed. His eyes were closed and he was nodding his head.

Then in the early morning I was woken by mother crying out, "Ah, he's gone. He's gone on us."

He was sitting up in bed exactly where I had left him. I put my hands on his two shoulders. He slumped forward, and when I eased him back he felt heavy and cold. His hands were colder still.

"Why didn't I stay with him? What tempted me to go to bed?" my mother said.

I tried pumping his chest. There was a groan. But it was only trapped air in the lungs.

It was somewhere between five and six o'clock in the morning and I laid him out straight in the bed and crossed his arms, but I did not cover his face. Then I left my mother alone with him in the bedroom.

The features of the countryside were still dark. I went directly to my brother Sean's house, tapped with a bare knuckle on the bedroom window-pane and called softly. He came to the front door and I spoke to him from the porch.

"It's Daddy," I said.

Next I drove into the village and knocked on the door of the priest's house. There was no answer. I felt I had been away a long time but I went to the telephone kiosk to try telephoning the priest. I got through straight away and he said he would be there as soon as he got dressed. On my way out of the kiosk three uniformed guards and a detective carrying an Uzi submachine gun stopped me.

They wanted to know my business. I had to avoid being 'obstreperous' with them and explain that my father was dead.

Once the priest had said the necessary prayers Sean's wife Catherine and Owen's wife Noreen set about tidying the house. We could expect callers soon and it was time to shave, wash and dress the corpse.

We went about the business of washing our dead father in a practical way. The odd groan of air still came from his lips. But we were level-headed, manly, determined. Traits he had taught us. I scrubbed his face with a cloth. We took turns with a bowl of water and a razor. Sean clipped his fingernails and tried removing years of nicotine stains.

He was sixty-four. Death had made him look younger. No longer straining to get the air that was all around him into his lungs, the features of his face were calm.

We had callers throughout the day but it was in the evening that the neighbours really began crowding in. The more people appeared the more numbing every dry handshake and well-meant "sorry for your trouble" became. But I did my best, standing alongside Uncle Joseph, my mother's younger brother. He had always admired my father. When it got dark he asked, "Do you need any messages?"

"No," said my mother.

"Are you sure? Not even a mineral?"

"Oh, for God's sake can't you let the man go for a pint," Sean's wife Catherine said. "He can bring back a few minerals."

If the people in the bar were surprised to see me and Joseph they did not show it. The pub regulars offered their condolences calling my father "A good man." "Likeable."

"A comical sort."

Then the conversation turned to the hunt for Dessie O'Hare, the 'Border Fox'. He had shot his way out of one police barracks already and was still on the loose despite a nationwide manhunt, the armed police checkpoints and the roving dawn patrols, one of which had intercepted me that morning.

"Your father never had much to say to the guards," Uncle Joseph said.

"Ná bí ag caint," I said, my father's words coming back to me.

And privately I thought about how annoyed I'd been when I got stopped outside the kiosk after calling the priest, knowing my mother was waiting on her own back at the house with my dead father. But I remembered what he said about 'a little bit of manners going a long way.' And the armed patrol turned out to be a great help, sending a message on the radio for a guard to accompany a neighbour to break the bad news to my brother Owen.

Uncle Joseph wiped away a big man's tears and said, "We'll dab." It was an expression my father used meaning it was time to go.

Outside the stars were shining brightly, the Big Dipper and the

Pole Star. And I thought of the charts of the night time sky my father had clipped out of the newspapers to teach me the constellations.

Back at the house my brothers Owen and Sean and I took our places in the bedroom to keep the traditional all-night family vigil over the corpse.

"If we really want to keep the old man company we should have a constant supply of Sweet Afton or Woodbine cigarettes burning in the ashtray and the clock radio tuned to Tommy O'Brien," Owen said.

We didn't go that far, but we had a few hot whiskeys with Uncle Joseph and drank beer from the neck of the bottle. We weren't the type to recite prayers, and my father would not have been the type to listen. Instead Owen had a story our neighbour Joan Murray told him earlier. She used to worry about an ass breaking into a field of ours beside her house. She put out the animal several times but he kept coming back. Finally, she met my father and told him about the thieving donkey.

"The old ass has to eat too," my father said. "Instead of putting him to the road, why don't you give the children a spin on his back?"

When the neighbours arrived to take our place in the early hours of the next morning they said we ought to get a couple of hours rest. But I couldn't sleep. Instead I changed into working clothes, built up the fire in the black Stanley Range in the kitchen and cleaned the ashes out of the grate in the front room; then went outside to do whatever jobs had to be done on the farm. The day was calm, the air stone-grey.

Later I went to the graveyard with a load of sandwiches, stout and whiskey for the men digging the grave. They had met a terrible rock and had been hammering away in turns at this intractable stone for hours. Owen and Sean had joined them and I took a turn too with the sledge hammer in the wet bottom of the family grave.

We were waist deep in the ground when Owen spotted a retired doctor walking between the headstones.

"Visiting his mistakes," Owen remarked, and our burst of laughter from the grave caught the doctor's attention. He came over to us, and there was "plenty of men looking at their wellingtons," said Owen, until he moved on. Then when we turned back to the rock at the bottom of the grave we saw how a hair-line crack had appeared. With a stroke of the hammer the stone broke perfectly in two.

Back at the house, the hardest moment came later that evening, when it was time to finally close the coffin and the screws shaped like tiny little crosses had to be fastened after the lid was put in place, closing off the last ever sight of my father. The priest sprinkled holy water with a besom over the coffin. I watched the specks of clear water gleam on the varnished wood. On the lid of the coffin the words "Rest in Pease" were engraved on a brass plaque, the word 'Peace' mistakenly spelled with an S. A detail that would not have escaped Daddy's notice. I pictured him giving me the wink and saying "Ná bí ag caint - the undertaker has to make a living, too."

# CUCKOO VISITS

I'VE TOLD CATHY SHE CAN EXPECT a two-storey farmhouse on the side of the mountain with stone-built barns, a hayshed, haggard, orchard and vegetable garden surrounded by hill fields so steep you could hang pictures on them.

Cathy will be meeting my mother for the first time.

I have a Black Forest Gateau with me, but I know my mother will already have an apple tart or a treacle cake made, and lunch prepared and left out in the back kitchen under a clean tea-towel, ready to be served. Home-made brown bread. Slices of ham folded in rolls on a bed of lettuce from her own garden, with short green scallions pulled too soon. Tomatoes. But not salad cream. She's been to America to see her sister and she prefers mayonnaise.

Cathy drives and we have two Dutch friends tailing us in their own car: two sisters in their late seventies, Constance and Jeannette.

Both women have the hallmarks of great beauty in their youth.

Jeannette has a knowing, travelled and self-effacing manner. Constance has strikingly observant bright eyes, wears a brooch at her neck, soft woollen cardigans and has the more notably brusque and aristocratic manner.

"You should change your hair," she said to Cathy the very first time they met. "Pick a good salon. Ask their advice. That's their job. Don't try to save money. Not on your hair."

I met Constance through her niece when I was travelling in the Netherlands. I've lost touch with the niece, but Constance and I have remained friends. When she arrived in Ireland last year I tried to repay her kindness to me in the Netherlands with a good impression of my home place. She met my mother and loved her.

"Your mother is wonderful," she said. "And so lively."

Now she wants her sister to meet her newly made friend in Ireland, and for Cathy the older women visitors are a welcome smokescreen.

I had telephoned earlier in the week to warn my mother we would be coming.

She would never forgive me if we caught her with the curlers in her hair, the sheets of newspaper left down on the kitchen floor after mopping or her kitchen table waiting to be cleared.

My mother comes out of the house to meet us. A small, mongrel terrier with a bunty-tail barks and then scuffles a welcome around our feet.

"She's the coldest dog in Ireland," my mother says. "She pushes past me in the morning to get in at the electric heater and takes all the heat. But she's company for me when I'm here on my own at night."

She talks non-stop as she leads us towards the house.

The green-cylinder push-mower has been in use on the neat lawn. Her daffodil and crocus flower beds are just coming into bloom. The greenhouse in the corner of the garden is stacked with polystyrene trays loaded with sprouting broccoli and early lettuce. And her "little man", a bare-bellied concrete cherub, stands in the other corner beside the conifer and heather bed, shouldering a bowl of flowering primula. A bushy azalea in a red earthenware pot is on display outside the porch.

When the women remark on its strong white blooms my mother says, "I've looked after it like a baby all winter. I'm in and out with it at night when there's a sign of frost. Slamming doors at all hours and waking up the neighbours."

There is a warm fire burning in the sitting room, which we have always called the lower room. The ladies are settled into big second-hand Dutch furniture chairs around the tiled fireplace. I seat Cathy on the sofa, leaving my mother to do all the talking.

After being complimented on her house she confides to her visitors that she gets ideas from visiting stately homes and fine gardens. Powerscourt is lovely, she tells Constance, but when she visited Bunratty Castle and saw its medieval interior she thought: "Bejesus, me own place is better than this."

I round up glasses from the china cabinet where the ornaments we bought for her as children are kept, and take the glasses to the back kitchen to pour a beer for myself, whiskey for the visitors and a sherry for my mother. I bring the drinks in on a tray. The glasses are raised and we say, "*Sláinte.*"

My mother says that Constance and Jeannette are a picture of health. They put it down to good fortune more than money. And my mother is reminded of a story about a woman of eighty-seven, living up the road on her own, who told a visiting Public Health Nurse she had neither an ache nor a pain despite her age, although at times her mind might wander a bit. When the Nurse asked what kind of food she had eaten over the years, she said: "Anything I was given."

Constance, having met my mother before, has a little story of her own ready.

"Jesus, Mary and Joseph were having a discussion about what places they would most like to visit if they were given a chance to return to this earth. Joseph said he'd love to go back to Nazareth to spend a day in the little carpenter's shop he'd had there. Jesus said he often longed to go back to the serenity and the peace he found around the sea of Galilee. Mary said that she'd love to pay a visit to the shrine at Knock, because she'd never been there before."

It's hard to say if my mother knows Constance is teasing.

"I left my hand on the spot where the apparition appeared," my mother says. "I used to have terrible pins and needles up and down my arm. The night after I got back I thought the pain in my arm was worse than ever. But when I woke up in the morning the pain was gone. It never came back."

Constance opens a shopping bag and produces a present for my mother: a framed photograph of a Marian Year shrine.

"I'm a great believer in the Blessed Virgin," my mother says, admiring the gift. "She always answers my prayers."

"The Irish are all great believers, I think, in the Blessed Virgin," Jeannette says.

"They're great believers in Saintly mothers," I suggest.

"Is it true that Irish men don't get married until late in life?" Jeannette asks Cathy.

"Married?" my mother says. "Why would they when they have the times of Molly Ban, with their mothers dancing attendance on them."

"There's an old joke," I say, "that Jesus must have been an

Irishman because his mother thought he was Christ Almighty."

"There's no religion in that buck," my mother says, leaving the photograph on the mantelshelf. "He takes that from his father, poor man..." Her words trail off.

"I miss him," she says, when Cathy asks. "He was a quiet sort. Too quiet, maybe. All I have against him is that he smoked himself to death. It was a selfish thing to do. He wasn't thinking about the rest of us."

The dog stretches out in its accustomed place on the rug in front of the fire. And Jeannette asks my mother if she has any regrets.

"It was a hard life," she says. "I always felt I had it hard, or at least I was always working, or taking care of someone. I took care of my father when he got sick, and I looked after my husband until the end."

I leave my mother chatting with the two older women and take Cathy outside for a look around the place.

The cows and the spring calves are in the pasture nearest the house. The farm machinery stands in the three-quarter empty hayshed. The mowing machine and hay turner have been left up since the winter and sit silent and stiff with rust. The grey diesel twenty tractor stands in the lane, as little used as the rest. I have already been back home for a week in April to fence off the meadows. Putting the cattle out of the meadows marks the start of another year saving hay. We will wait for the meadows to fill with clover, long grass and wildflowers, and then keep a close eye on the long-range weather forecast, and when the computer charts, satellite photos and isobars say the Gulf Stream has edged into Northern waters, and a ridge of high pressure is on the way, we will make hay.

I walk with Cathy to the meadow gate. The hawthorn hedges are in green leaf, with just a week or so to wait for their bridal veils of white blossom.

"So your mother has to run things by herself if you're not here?" Cathy says.

"She knows more about the animals than the rest of us put together. And we keep the herd number down to what she can manage."

"Isn't it hard work for her?"

"She'd rather be farming than stuck in the house all day."

"Would you consider taking over?"

"I don't think any one of us wants to be tied down to the place."

From the uppermost branches of a big sycamore tree at the end of the meadow field we hear a cuckoo calling. We listen to its cuckoo calls, home again for the summer and seeking out a mate.

Back at the house Cathy smiles at me when she sees the ham, tomatoes, lettuce and young scallions I'd predicted. Everyone has to plead with my mother to sit and join us at the table.

Cathy asks her about my brothers.

"Both married and gone," my mother tells her. "There's only this fella left."

"It's only natural that they leave," Constance reassures my mother while smiling at Cathy. "They outgrow the nest. And leaving is a good thing. Like planting out your seedlings – it toughens them up."

We have a lovely afternoon, and then the two Dutch women say they would prefer not to have to drive after dark. I show them the best way to turn their car around in the farmyard and my mother, who has never driven a car in her life, tells Cathy to be sure to take the lane in first gear.

A commotion starts when the dog notices the cattle and their young calves wandering into the lane ahead of the cars. My mother runs up the lane and waves her arms to herd the slow-moving cattle out of the way.

"I think your mother panicked," Cathy says, watching my mother run the cattle back towards the pasture. We beep the horn and wave farewell through the open windows of the car, and looking back I see my mother standing by her cattle and growing slighter with distance as I lead the visitors out the gate.

# THE LAKE OF BRIGHTNESS

YOU WERE OUR FIRST CALLER to our first house that first summer in Dromahair. We'd bought a gamekeeper's cottage a meadow field away from the Bonet River that flows into Lough Gill – from the Irish, meaning the lake of brightness.

Welcoming, gallant and eager, the boat trip was your idea; the weather being fabulous, with Gulf Stream warm seas, dolphins and giant sunfish off the West Coast. While inland the dogs drank like fish and the fish sweated like dogs.

We sloughed off work and slapped on sun lotion, thinking of this gloriously unreal spell as Gatsby's Lawn: a charmed dreamtime to play house, to enjoy life, to live with our eyes closed to heartbreak. Not recognising another parallel with Gatsby: that something preyed on you, a 'foul dust' floating in the wake of your readiness to join us in living for the moment.

For the boat trip we packed the cool-box with salads, soft cheese and hardboiled eggs, bread, salami, wine and delectable summer strawberries. You brought the can of petrol for the outboard.

You had this mongrel black fibreglass boat designed along the lines of an Aran Island currach. It was capable of taking a half-ton load and steady as a barge with cargo. But it felt plastic and bouncy without ballast and at first the engine stalled, unwilling to be press ganged into pleasure cruising.

You plucked the cord again and again until the propeller spun and we took to the open water with not enough life jackets to go around if we came to grief.

Heat haze made the countryside blue as the inside of a fresh-water muscle shell. Sunlight bounced off the bright water, and beyond the shoreline and the summery uplands, the far mountains formed the contours of a 'Sleeping Giant', the points of his boots and his smooth round forehead resting peacefully in a blanket of baby blue haze.

We passed the famous Lake Isle of Innisfree that you said was only 'a clump of bushes'. Arriving instead on Church Island, we rolled out the rug in a sunlit pasture full of clover and the smell of bluebell pollen. Then you stripped off for a dip, letting out yelps of scalded delight plunging into the lap of the serenely inviting lake.

You were a determined and a competitive swimmer. But when your head surfaced suddenly I noticed your neck ringed by ripples like portents, now in hindsight, of the noose you would fashion with such careful ingenuity when the black wave of depression took you under.

In the backwash of your suicide our grief was terrible, thinking back on that lovely summer and the boat trip; the blissful weather, the enchanted setting, our risk taking happiness in a strange craft suspend on a glassy membrane of bright water over a dark and cruel kingdom of citizens lost to the deep forever.

# ONE SMALL STEP .

On the 15th January 1999, a controlled explosion toppled the Arigna power station chimney. The end of this trim smokestack on the lip of Lough Allen, the first lake fed from the headwaters of the Shannon Pot, was a calculated demolition job sanctioned by the Electricity Supply Board, having found the chimney a safety hazard in need of tearing down.

It appeared a gratuitous act: the chimney being such a conspicuous landmark in an area with a newfound interest in promoting its industrial heritage. And it hadn't escaped local notice either that the chimney weathered the severe storms over the Christmas seemingly without a problem. Adding fuel to the suspicion the chimney had to come down because the ESB feared deregulation; one day a competitor might re-commission the old generating station to burn Arigna's remaining coal reserves, which were paltry according to informed sources, and plentiful according to the conspiracy theorists.

My reasons for missing the power station chimney were typically more obscure.

I was born in 1960, the year the French started nuclear testing and the British launched their Dreadnought nuclear submarine.

Throughout my childhood the Pentagon and the Kremlin kept their nuclear arsenals on a war footing where ten minutes was all it would take to get their Intercontinental Ballistic Missiles, or ICBM's, off the launch pads aimed at the strategic bulls-eyes of Eastern and Western Europe.

Younger people nowadays can hardly imagine the climate of constant dread in which we grew up. The Soviet nuclear arsenal alone had the capacity to kill 22,000.million people, on a planet with a total human population at the time of just under 4,000.million people. Given the cosmic magnitude of the threat you could no more ignore the prospect of nuclear extinction, than the man Martin Amis describes with 'the cocked gun in his mouth who may boast that he never thinks about the cocked gun. But he tastes it, all the time.'

And then in October 1962, both Khrushchev and Kennedy found themselves locked into nuclear confrontation when American spy planes spotted Soviet missile bases in Cuba. Alarmed US Forces mounted a blockade around their renegade neighbour while Soviet warships steamed towards the blockade for a showdown, and the world's first mass television audience watched helplessly transfixed by the escalating prospect of all out Armageddon.

Both sides eventually backed down, but having narrowly escaped an atom bomb fuelled World War III, Irish policy makers took decisive action. They issued every household in the country with a booklet.

The Civil Defence booklet had flimsy green covers, and was printed in black and red ink on grainy cheap paper. The thinking behind it was to prepare you for the morning when, looking out your kitchen window you saw a gargantuan atomic mushroom cloud swelling over the horizon from a nuclear bomb being dropped on the Irish countryside. In the unlikely event that you survived this first strike detonation, the blast wave, and the ensuing nuclear firestorm with the power to reduce you and everyone belonging to you to scorch marks on the inside of any concrete wall that might be left standing, then there were certain steps the booklet recommended.

The cinders of God's creation would now be drifting down on your head in the form of radioactive ashes. And this toxic fallout was represented in the booklet as red blotches dotted on the leaves of big heads of cow cabbage and draped along the spines of cattle in the fields: so you should therefore avoid eating cabbage or beef.

The same red dot radiation was shown to slant in windows at an exact forty-five degree angle, and householders who hadn't the foresight to convert their one-off concrete septic tanks into nuclear fall-out shelters stocked with canned food and uncontaminated drinking water, were advised to remove a household door from its hinges and prop it under the window at an equivalent forty-five degree angle to the incoming radiation. Then cowering under the door for protection you ought to assume the best position in the event of a nuclear attack – crouch down, place your head between your knees and 'kiss your ass goodbye'.

Useless in the event of all out nuclear war, that booklet haunted my imagination. Every time I looked up at a jet vapour trail tracking across the sky I wonder what if it turned out to be the first in a wave of nuclear warheads. And on the farm my brothers and I became obsessed with building hide-outs. Maybe it was the subconscious influence of living in a coal mining valley. But I put it down to that booklet. We never built tree-houses, we dug bunkers. My older brother excavated a huge hole in the corner of a pasture field and roofed it with sheets of galvanized iron. He called it the "trite". It was strictly private and reserved for him and his school friends. I was too young for admission and so I found a dank and draughty alternative under the dark eye of a railroad bridge that was in every regard, batty. My younger brother got a spade and dug a damp, child-sized hole in the earth, which, roofed with branches and sods, looked exactly like he'd dug his own grave and crawled into it.

Mercifully the world superpowers saw that using their missiles offensively could only ever produce one result: Mutual Assured Destruction or MAD for short. So they opted for a balance of terror whereby the missiles sulked in their silos, always fuelled, always primed: ever on hand as a nuclear deterrent.

A standoff that prompted a neighbour of ours, Tom Packie, looking towards the missile-like Arigna power station chimney, 'That's what this country needs – our own nuclear detergent'.

Tom Packie had been in England at the tail end of the Second World War when the rockets called Doodlebugs began to hit London. The Doodlebugs he said, made a droning noise that would put the heart crossways in you, but they were even more deadly when they went silent, after the rocket engine cut out and their explosive payload went into freefall.

Those cunning Doodlebugs ushered in the age of rocket engines as tactical weapons.

And then the Russians launched Sputnik, and shot Yuri Gagarin into orbit, truly getting the space race started. Kennedy responded saying, 'We choose the moon'. And unashamedly dependent on

Wernher Von Braun's ill-gotten Doodlebug and V2 rocket science, the Americans got their own Apollo moonshot underway. So that by the time I was nine years old the power station chimney in Arigna was no longer a fuming ICBM in my imagination but a Saturn V Rocket on the launch pad at Cape Canaveral.

Unlike today's ramshackle space shuttle, the Apollo rockets were marvellously elegant at rest and magisterial on take off. Their upward thrust and staged separations choreographed by the Huston control centre had a balletic grace that fitted the epoch defining Apollo 11 takeoff with its three astronauts ascending towards the moon on a golden balloon of burning rocket fuel.

By the evening of July 20th 1969, Kennedy had been slain in Dallas and his widow, once married to the most powerful man on the face of the earth was now married to the richest man on the waves. Arigna Collieries had closed for their summer holidays from July 12th to the 29th. And after several weeks of indifferent weather the sunshine was back. It was the last night of the Festival of the Shannon and Jeanette Dunne had earlier won a prize for her fancy dress as Jackie Onassis at Phil the Fluters Ball.

Sean Dunphy and the Hoedowners were playing in the Mayflower Ballroom in Drumshanbo.

But the fact that you could rent a television from McDermotts in Carrick-on-Shannon for nine and six per week meant that most people were at home glued to their black and white sets.

Earlier we'd watched *Daniel Boone* and the *Lucy Show*. Coverage of the moonlanding would start at nine o' clock.

Alongside the single RTE channel listing in the *Leitrim Observer* there was a picture of a child with a hunger bloated belly and an appeal for donations to assist a famine-stricken Biafra. Another advertisement said, 'If your grandson calls a biscuit a cookie isn't it time you had a word with him'. And beneath the slogan the Aer Lingus Shamrock Jet fleet offered flights every day to the US and Canada.

But our thoughts were concentrated on Michael Collins, minding the mother craft, and Buzz Aldrin and Neil Armstrong steering towards the Sea of Tranquilly. The Eagle had landed, but then the door got stuck. And I was heavy-eyed with sleep by the time Neil Armstrong finally hopped down the metal ladder in his spacesuit and stamped the corrugated track of his boot in the lunar dust.

He may or may not have fluffed his line, that this was 'one small step for a man, one giant leap for mankind'. But it didn't matter. A bigger television audience than ever watched the Cuban missile crisis cheered the bravery of these astronauts, and shared in the tension of an endeavour at the limits of human ingenuity. And when my eyes turned heavenwards once more the moon had become a looking glass reflecting an altogether more hopeful, sweet old world.

# FLORIDA COAST

ALL SHE HAD EATEN since she got up was a crust of brown bread with a scrape of orange marmalade and a mug of hot tea. Hot tea was an addiction, coloured with milk and sweetened with a half-spoon of sugar. It cured her headaches in the morning and helped her relax when she was alone in the house at night.

Her guts were rattling but the morning jobs were done, and she was pulling off her waterproofs and wellington boots when the telephone in the kitchen rang and the caller said, "Hello, Tess."

It was her sister Maureen.

"It's great to hear your voice," she said. "You must have known I was thinking about you."

"Is everything all right?"

"When were things ever all right in Ireland? How is everybody in America?"

"We're all fine. Joseph and his wife were up for a few days from Chicago, and I had our old neighbour from home Molly and her husband George Oliver over."

"I thought that man was dead and buried."

"I had them stay with me for a couple of days. It was just like old times."

"Visitors can be a big strain, Maureen, especially if you're the one doing all the entertaining. You must be worn out."

"Are you kidding? I enjoyed getting in from work and finding someone in the house. The place is so empty since Susan got married. Especially at night – we've all kinds of lousy bums and weirdoes now hanging around the old neighbourhood."

"I've got a few hops here on my own. Last night I thought I heard someone outside walking past the window."

"Did you call the cops?"

"It was only a badger," she said. "But he put the heart crossways in me."

It would have upset her sister in America too much if she confessed how severely her courage had been tested and how she'd barely slept a wink the whole night after the incident.

"Why don't you come over, Tess?"

"You know I can't get away."

"What's holding you? The boys are married and have their own lives now. You're a widow same as me. And you've never been to the house in Florida."

"It's a rest I need, Maureen, not travel. I'm cold and I'm tired the whole time. I'd want to put horse-nails in my soup I'm so short of iron."

"You've got to look after your health. I'll buy vitamins and we'll drive down to Clearwater. You can pick your own oranges in the back garden and juice them. How does that sound?"

"God, I don't know, Maureen."

"I'll send you the dollars. Or I can book the trip from here and send the ticket."

"It's not the expense."

"What's holding you then?"

"The cattle."

"Sell the lousy cattle!"

She felt the tips of her ears heat up. "Someone has to look after the farm, Maureen," she said. "It's not just the cattle. If I don't keep the bracken down the weeds will take over. So I cut a square every dry hour I get. It's thankless work, I know. Like dusting and cleaning the house, it doesn't stay done long. But it has to be done all the same."

"Ask some of the boys to come back and look after the place for a while."

"They have their own lives, Maureen."

"What about the neighbours?"

How could she explain to her sister that animals were like small children: most people would volunteer to look after them for a day or two, but not for a week or a fortnight.

"It's very good of you to ask, Maureen, but you'll have to let me think about it. Why don't I write? This call must be costing you a fortune."

"I'm not worried about the price of a phone call," Maureen said, trying to mask the note of frustration in her voice

"I don't see how I can get away. The barn needs a new door. And I had the expense of putting in the phone this year."

"I told you not to worry about the money. I'll pay for the trip."

"I'll have to wait until the spring calves are stronger."

"I'll send you the dollars anyway."

"I'll only send them back."

"O for Christ's sake, what's a few lousy bucks? I'll call again in a week."

She was beginning to regret ever having answered the call, and the moment she put the hand-set back in the cradle she said to herself, "Now what am I going to do?"

In the back of the cupboard in the kitchen she kept an album bulging with old photographs taken mainly in America. Tess and Maureen's mother, Annie McDaid had worked in a candy store and ice-cream parlour in Manhattan on East 23rd Street in Jazz Age New York. The business was owned by Scottish relations, and the ice-cream parlour was really a front for selling bootleg gin and beer during Prohibition. Annie was the sweet young colleen, fresh from the old country, who served the children candies while the owner out the back filled the lidded quart cans the children carried with beer to bring home to their parents.

As soon as she could, Annie left New York and came home with a massive elephant-hide trunk full of coats and dresses, and a war-chest of savings to buy land and a dowry to get married. By the start of the 1950s, her older teenage daughter, Maureen, was ready to book passage back to America to repeat the same plan.

From the moment Maureen arrived she loved the United States, and she soon encouraged her younger brother Joseph to quit the coalmines and join her. He did a stint in the coalmines of Pittsburgh and then Maureen brought him to New York to help put him through evening trades classes in Queens where he qualified as an electrician and got himself into a union, eventually finishing up in

Chicago.

Maureen hadn't only helped her brother get settled in America, she'd sent a portion of her wages back to Ireland every time she got paid to help her parents build a new two-storey farmhouse to replace the original three-room cottage under the sycamores. Out of every pay check she earned Maureen sent a certain amount home, even after she got married and had children of her own to rear and educate.

She was a shy girl who never owned a bathing suit; she'd visit the beach, but only in a summer frock and high heels. She started to go out with a young man but then dropped him after seeing what she called, 'The hump on him on a barstool'. Instead she married Jack Donlon, and their social life revolved around dinner dances given by the Armagh and Roscommon peoples' associations: linen and silver-service occasions with her new husband Jack looking thrilled, and Maureen at his side beaming with happy bedazzlement and emigrant pride.

Maureen and Jack's hard work ethic allowed them to set their sites on retiring to Florida where they bought a house near St Petersburg. And one time Maureen proposed to fly to Florida from New York with a tray of her homemade lasagne on her lap to welcome Irish visitors. She got her way at the airport and all went well until the plane hit turbulence.

Then, before either Maureen or Jack could retire to Florida Jack developed cancer and died, and Maureen decided to keep on working.

A few years ago Maureen needed a triple heart by-pass. When the surgeon broke the news she fought tooth and nail with him to avoid surgery that would require a long period of rest. She wanted medication instead. But on learning she wasn't a suitable candidate, the very next time the surgeon made his rounds Maureen asked, "When's my operation?"

"Oh," he said, "so now you're in a hurry."

She visited Florida when she could, though she found it a lonesome journey without Jack, and to get the trip behind her one time she set out after a wedding in New York to drive the whole way with nobody to share the driving and no overnight stop.

She had no memory whatsoever of the last part of the trip, crossing in a daze the vast Howard Frankland Bridge that joins

Tampa and St. Petersburg.

Digging deep into her willpower and long-haul stamina, pure determination brought her at last to her dream retirement home in Florida. The one with the orange trees in the garden – a sight to gladden her eyes after such a phenomenal journey, and a confirmation to herself she'd made it in the end.

Tess sifted through the photographs and found one of Maureen and Jack standing in the front room of their fine home on Long Island. There were books and pictures of the Catskill Mountains on the walls in place of the holy pictures and 'Missionary Order' calendars found at home. Jack wore a dinner suit and Maureen wore a white fur-collar-trimmed coat, elbow-length gloves and a lovely string of pearls.

The photographs from home were different, and she paused to look at one of herself and her mother in sturdy foursquare buttoned coats. She looked dowdy and bedraggled and stuck at home compared with Maureen in her pearls, and the only sign of prosperity was an antique car with a rusty hole eaten in the driver's door.

Strange then how the ones who got on so well in America never really broke the connection with the old world. And the first chance they got they either came home on holiday or wanted the family members in Ireland to come over to them. "The place will be there when you get back," Maureen often said, doing her best to inveigle Tess to come to the U.S. And she had made the trip once or twice, with Maureen collecting her at JFK Airport and looking after her like Royalty.

But now they were both widowed and both living alone, one in the States and one in Ireland. Neither of them was getting any younger, and Maureen was contemplating retirement from the Postal Service, while Tess privately knew how hard it was to keep the farm on the mountain going by herself.

She was ready to put away the album when a picture of her brother Joseph holding a hayfork up high on a brilliant summer's day slipped out from between the pages. Standing beside Joseph was their father Henry Joe McDaid wearing a scruffy hat, a waistcoat and collarless shirt with the sleeves rolled up.

At the height of the hay saving weather one summer's morning, Joseph and their father Henry Joe had been carrying their pitchforks to the meadow field with the whole hard hay-saving day ahead of them, when two American women arrived in an open-top car so big it took up almost the entire width of the laneway to the farmhouse.

The older of the two women was a widow called Nancy Regan. And she was travelling with her daughter, Joy.

"Hi there," Joy called out to the pair of farmers, and she explained how she and her mother were looking for their ancestors.

"The Regan family?" said Henry Joe, shoving his hat back on his head. It was already a roasting hot day and there was a line of sweat along the headband. As far as he knew there had been no family by the name of Regan living on that part of the mountain for at least five generations. But he felt a small deception would be better than outright disappointment.

"All that's left of the Regan's old family home is right there," he said pointing to the cow barn.

Thatched, whitewashed and aged, it was the humble birthplace Molly and her daughter Joy had always imagined. And after the pictures were taken, Nancy produced a wad of dollars to compensate for the disruption to the work.

"Put that money back in your pocketbook," Henry Joe said firmly.

"But you must have something," Molly insisted.

Joy said they were headed for the seaside and there was plenty of room in the car if the men wanted an outing. Joseph had not taken his eyes off Joy's bright open face and twists of California sun-gold hair. And wearing a plaid shirt and baggy working pants that highlighted his athletic build, Joy had also been eyeing up Joseph. Molly too found Henry Joe entertaining company.

Joseph of course would have downed tools on the spot to take up the women's offer, but Henry Joe said, "We have a field of hay down."

The field of hay had been cut four days ago by the hired man with the fingerboard mowing machine, and the wet lumps of green hay were then scattered by hand and turned twice with wooden hay-rakes. It was time to get the field of hay saved.

And of all the people the women could meet, Henry Joe was one of the most conscientious farmers around when it came to fixing the roof of the thatched barn, or building a turf-stack properly to hold out the rain. He was especially particular about the quality of the hay he saved each year, and working in the meadow field he took longer than most men to build a cock of hay. Each haycock had to be neatly layered and made to stand straight as a plumb-line, the sides carefully groomed with the wooden hay rake, the top headed off with a cap of greener hay delicately shaken out with the pitchfork, the butt trimmed by hand, and the surplus used to make hay ropes with the twister as each handsome haycock was tied at the base to hold it down through the most unforeseen summer squall.

So while Henry Joe opened the gate into the meadow field, Joy and Molly followed in the rented car, giving Joseph a ride in the back as he showed them the best place to turn around the big car with the automatic gear shift. Then they waited for Henry Joe to make a determination on the fitness of the hay for saving.

The summer sun shone down from a cloudless blue sky. A warm breeze fragrant with sweetly seasoned hay stirred the burnished wisps at his feet. Henry Joe picked up a handful of hay so dry it practically broke into chaff. He looked across at Joseph sitting at the wheel where Joy was encouraging him to do a test drive, and then at Molly patting and fixing her hair with a little brush she returned to the handbag holding the stout pocketbook. He thought about the sea and a change of air and he released his grip and said, "It needs another day."

In Florida it was so hot the pavement would burn the soles of your feet. But just as Maureen had promised there were mango and orange trees growing in the garden when Tess got out of the car in front of her sister's house in Clearwater. She wore a broad brimmed straw hat and sunglasses and a light cotton summer dress. She was getting used to these hot latitudes. Although, when they were skirting Tallahassee on the drive from Long Island, she had ordered tea at an air-conditioned diner. The waitress brought iced tea in a tall glass with a drinking straw and a paper umbrella. As the girl who'd served her this concoction retreated she said to Maureen: "I'll have to bring her into the kitchen and show her how to boil a kettle."

For the next ten days they had a lovely time together. The holiday took the chill out of her old bones and she loved the fresh orange juice every morning made from fruit picked off the trees in the back garden. Maureen could not have been a kinder or a more generous host.

But everything is always about something else. And towards the end of the holiday Maureen made it clear she wanted Tess to move to

Florida. She urged her not to be killing herself looking after the home place. She should sell the damn cattle and rent out the land and stop farming altogether. Maureen would help her with the move. She would take care of Tess in America and she wanted nothing in return only her sister's company.

Tess said she appreciated everything Maureen was doing for her but she would need time to think about it. Florida had a lot of good points. Food and clothes were cheap. The place had every kind of facility for retired people. It was a tempting offer.

On the other hand she knew from the time she spent with her own Active Age group learning to play golf, taking flower-arranging and basket weaving classes, how hard it is to keep yourself amused. She'd much rather be farming and doing something useful. So she told Maureen she'd give her final answer only after she got back.

She had no fear of flying but her stomach was queasy with nervous indecision when they got to the airport. The Americans she'd met were lovely, and she couldn't put her finger on why she felt so anxious at the prospect of moving full-time to the United States to be with her sister.

Then after Maureen had seen her off at 'Departures' there was an incident at the airport. She had a lot on her mind and she was slow to get her passport out and holding up the line when a big security guard with a gun on his hip came over and told her. "Mam, keep moving…. Keep moving, mam…."

When the flight arrived at Dublin airport there was an Irish guard behind a window who had to see everyone's passport on the way out. Again she had to open her coat and reach into her cardigan and root around in her clothes until the guard who was waiting for her to find her passport said, "You have it well hidden anyway." And she knew in heart she was home.

# DEEP DOWN

I know the road like the back of my hand, but still I find it tricky giving directions to strangers to the 'Arigna Mining Experience'. Most first-time visitors get lost along the way. I've even heard how a car-load of German tourists stopped and asked a couple of the lads cutting grass in the graveyard on Chapel Hill – known as the 'dead centre' of Arigna – for directions to the 'mining museum'.

"Do you see that lorry coming down into the valley," the German tourists were told, "if it was going the other way you could follow it straight there."

It doesn't matter if you get lost looking for the place; the scenery makes up for the inconvenience. Unlike the Welsh and English coalmines, found deep in the valleys, the Arigna mines stand on elevated sites.

Technically speaking they're not mineshafts; they're 'adits', or headings, driven straight into the hillsides to follow horizontal coal-beds sandwiched in narrow seams between the shale and sandstone.

So when I started working in Arigna as a young coalminer I never had to contend with that daunting plunge deep into the bowels of the earth found in English or American mines. In Pittsburgh though, where I was a miner for a while, a pal from Arigna who'd come with me wrote home and said we'd just sunk a shaft so deep 'the bottom fell out of it'.

Arigna today is like the rest of the country in places where heavy industry has made way for heritage industry. The mines, the mills and factories, and the related machinery and hand tools, have all been taken out of common use and labelled and preserved behind glass. The relics of what Sean Lemass once envisioned as an industrial base for a modern Ireland neither makes nor does anything useful anymore: in its place we have visitor centres, coffee shops and toilet stops. It's progress of a sort. And when I'm back home from Chicago on holiday it gives me somewhere to go; even if I never thought I'd live to see the day when I'd pay money to go down a mine.

In all fairness, they've done a nice job on the place. The car park occupies the levelled crest of a spoil-heap from the mine that anyone from Arigna only ever called the 'Bing'; a word that like a lot of the mining expertise in Arigna originally came from Scotland.

Set back from the car park, the buildings that houses the Mining Experience looks like a set of metal pyramids ingeniously suggesting they are part of something larger: the leading edges of three massive iron cubes tilted to extend underground.

But it's not the view from the car-park across counties Roscommon, Leitrim, Sligo, Longford and Cavan, or those clever iron pyramids, or the exhibits within, or the coffee shop and relief for the bladder and my dodgy prostate, that has practically everyone I've talked to afterwards saying how emotional they found their visit. The clincher for most people is the tour underground. It gives people the chance to experience at first hand what life was truly like for men like me when we worked at the coalface.

I use the word 'truly' with a slight reservation, because the section of mine re-opened to the public has to meet stringent health and safety standards that certainly didn't apply to the original coalmine when I worked there as a young man. The height of the roof has been raised, there are heavy duty steel girders – not softwood props – holding up the roof; there's bright electric light, a generally even surface underfoot, and good ventilation. And yet, even though you are as near as is humanly possible to one hundred percent safe, most people still need to gather their courage to leave behind the comforting daylight above ground.

It's this feeling of unease as you first stop into the mine that makes the experiences authentic. Straight away you sense the unusualness of the job.

Often as not, this troubling sensation prompts visitors to take another look at the photograph of the Arigna miner who appears on the promotional banners, billboards, and at least one version of the attraction's brochure.

It's not me; he's several years younger.

His name is Eugene McPartland. And if you look at his right hand he's carrying the kind of pit helmet and lamp every one of us used back then. He has his jacket draped over his shoulders and his chest is exposed with a safety-pin holing the front of his shirt closed. His hands, face and chest are smudged with coal dust and grime. Even so, I've heard him referred to as a 'fine thing'; and he is certainly a striking figure: the quintessential Arigna coalminer who happened to have his picture taken on what for any one of us would have been the end of a normal eight-hour shift. He is on his way home while dressed in his working clothes, or as he'd have called them himself, his 'pit duds'.

When that photograph was taken, Eugene would have been just one amongst several hundred homeward headed pitmen, every one of us covered in coal dust from our scalps to the soles of our feet. And it was the sight of several hundred men with our coal-dust blackened faces and flashing white eyes trooping home in the dusk in helmets and heavy boots that gave the place where I grew up its strangeness and its character. For after a hard day in the pit, likely as not, we would be making straight for Flynn's pub after work or Wynn's pub in Drumkeeran, or Shivnan's in Ballyfarnon for a pint to 'wash down the dust'.

The first time my brother-in-law Jack Donlon, who was home on holiday from America, came to Arigna he was enjoying a quiet drink in Shivnan's bar in Ballyfarnon when he spotted the owner pulling pint after pint of stout in the otherwise empty bar. He kept filling drinks until he had a whole long line of pints stretching the entire length of the bar counter – 'cooking' as he called letting the draft Guinness settle. Then shortly after four o'clock, the door burst open and in rushed a pack of pitmen with a line of creamy pints ready and waiting for them, their thirst urgent and their custom dependable.

And while one lot of coal miners paid for their drinks with damp and grimy banknotes from being carried around all day in working trousers and jacket pockets, another lot of pitmen came in and threw back a quick pint and 'half-one' before heading in the opposite direction to work on the back-shift from four until midnight.

We had no facilities you see for getting scrubbed up or hosed down either before or after work; you togged out in your pit-clothes at home before going to work and you wore them home again in the evening. And even though we grumbled and there were sudden walk-outs and industrial strikes over the primitive conditions and unsanitary arrangements, after another small pay rise on the part of the mine owners the showers were forgotten until the next dispute.

The lack of showers was only ever a secondary issue in the history of Arigna's industrial disputes. Though that's not to deny how over the years small matters of pride and principle often escalated from spontaneous walkouts into bitter and extended standoffs between the pitmen and the pit owners.

We had some long, hard, bitter strikes over the years where it was important to hold our ground, but even if it was only a few hotheads responsible for a walk-out you were obliged to support them. Men who broke the strike lived the rest of their days with the name of being 'scabs' and little in the way of thanks from the owners. There was even an attempt one time by the clergy to hold a women's ballot, to get the women to vote for the men to go back to work. Families were split and in some families the divisions never healed.

Though that's not to say we didn't have our own fun on the miner's marches led by a Pipe Band to Carrrick-on-Shannon with a stop along the way for 'refreshments' in Leitrim village where the likes of Packie Duignan would give us a tune .

And when I think about our miner's strikes in the 60's and 70's and 80's, it's like turning back the clock to a forgotten era of nearly constant industrial unrest. You had bank strikes that left people penniless because they couldn't cash a cheque, and ESB strikes that regularly left everyone without current; unofficial and official strike actions and marches by ordinary workers protesting at the outrageously high rates of PAYE, and farmers' marches too over what were seen as ruinous common agricultural policy agreements. Nearly every trade union in Ireland followed the example of Britain, where British Leland car makers were so rarely seen working on the assembly line it was said 'they only showed up to sign the visitors' book'. Militant trade unionism grew so engrained even in Arigna that when one of the lads innocently remarked 'I see the daffodils are out,' the pitman working alongside him said, 'Is it official or unofficial?'

In the long run of course the trade union movement suffered a pulverising defeat when Margaret Thatcher broke the miners' strike led by Arthur Scargill – a man I remember most, not for his doomed clash with Thatcherism, but for the way he dealt with a representative of British Nuclear Fuels who compared a small capsule containing a radioactive isotope with a nugget of coal the same size and spoke of the massive potential energy from such a tiny amount of nuclear material against the miniscule amount of energy that might be derived from the same sized piece of coal. Unfazed, Scargill took the piece of coal from his opponent's hand and swallowed it. 'Now try that with yours,' he told the agent promoting Nuclear Fuels.

Not that the mining of coal was free from danger: in fact the proponents of nuclear energy generation can rightly point out that on a worldwide basis many more human lives have been lost mining coal than have been lost through nuclear energy mishaps.

A fundamental difference between British coalmines and the pits in Arigna, though, was the absence of naturally occurring gas. We never had to contend with the violent explosions and fires that resulted from the build up of these underground gases in mines elsewhere in the world.

Cave-ins, gas explosions and flooding were less likely to cost me my life working in the Arigna mines than everyday carelessness – such as using a vice-grip on a moving crank rather than the required safety handle which is how one man lost his arm, or accidentally falling into a coal bunker that cost another man his life. All the same, the working conditions were primitive and physical injuries inevitable. So it should come as no surprise that even the most unconcerned Arigna miner, at the start of their working day in the pit, stopped to say a prayer in front of the picture of the Sacred Heart with the red bulb burning a short distance inside the entrance.

It made sense to stop at the picture of Jesus, as one old miner warned me on my first day underground, because, he said, "you could be talking to the man himself before the day is out".

Lung and breathing difficulties were the main illnesses, caused by the coal dust, and the damp compressed air underground, and aggravated too by cigarettes and farmer's lung. And in Arigna you always had more widows than old pitmen. But even on a day to day basis it took a particular kind of bravery to spend your working day in confined spaces in dark, wet tunnels prone to rock falls and jagged stone wedges, or 'bullets', as we called them, jutting down out of the roof of the pit that even wearing a helmet could leave you seeing stars if you banged your head off one of them.

Even with a good carbide light you had to pick your steps with care amongst jack-legged air picks, rattling steel ropes, coal cutting machines, compressed air hoses, hutches loaded with coal, the reek from burning fuse wire and spent gelignite, pockets of smothering 'black damp' and the blare and reverberation of controlled explosions, the force of these underground explosions controlled, it should be said, by men like me who left school at the ages of fourteen and fifteen to work in the pits, yet had the dexterity to measure the precise amount of explosives needed to clear the coalface and not cave in that whole section of tunnel or even bring down the roof of the entire mine.

Most daunting of all, was to find yourself stranded in the dark, alone in the subterranean chill and savage blackness of a mineshaft. Electric lamps came later, and even then many of the older miners disliked their heavy and cumbersome rechargeable batteries. Instead they maintained carbide and water lamps – beautifully made though often battered brass lamps with circular reflectors blacked from use – the nuggets of carbide going in the bottom compartment and the water supply in the top, the gradual drip of the water onto the calcified carbide releasing acetylene gas.

I always took great pride in keeping the flame adjusted and the trickle of water regulated to produce a clear and non-smutty light to work by. Though you could still run out of carbide and find yourself badly stranded in a lightless branch of the mine.

Men would keep stashes of carbide hidden in a waterproof tin in case of just such an emergency. And for fun I was often the prime culprit stealing a stranded pitman's hidden supply. Then I'd wait in the dark to hear the reaction. There was one man, and you wouldn't slip the blade of a small knife between the 'effing and the blinding' when he found his carbide taken. He lit the road with curses.

You might run short of carbide underground, but the water was always plentiful. Yet the retired miners who lead the tours today will dismiss this chilly iron-tainted water that plagued and thwarted every move we made underground. Even the thirstiest miner wouldn't touch it, because the superstition said if you drank pit water your skin would break out in boils.

For the bulk of visitors today, though, it is seeing how we worked lying on our backs on narrow ledges hacking at thin veins of coal and massive slabs of rock through which that tainted ground water teemed into your jacket cuffs and down the ridge of your back, which most starkly brings home the harshness of our lives. The tight confinement in the dark while simultaneously getting soaked to the skin as you worked, being the price you paid to earn a living at the coalface.

All told you had over three hundred men who genuinely knew the rough and the funny side of life underground: men with the ability to keep at bay the natural human dread of dark confined spaces while at the same time able to apply the intuitive mixture of brute force and ingenuity needed for the commercial transit of coal to the surface of the earth.

This larger business of extracting prehistorically formed coal from the Upper Carboniferous mountains of Arigna meant there was money and jobs in Arigna when few places in Ireland could offer worthwhile paid employment, and there was a time when it was thought that having a job in the coalmines of Arigna was as good as winning the Sweepstakes.

I bumped into a lovely couple the other day, Alice Maher and Dermot Seymour. I told them I was Joseph McDaid and I'd been a miner before I went to America, and that while it was sad to see the mines closed I was glad no son of mine would ever have to work in the pit. We got talking about fishing and the photograph in The Miners Bar showing a bunch of Arigna pitmen proudly brandishing a massive wedge of coal for the camera. Dermot said it was the exact same way a fisherman would sport a specimen catch. And it made me realise that whatever hardship the pitmen of Arigna might have endured over the years it never quenched their pride.

Though pride alone doesn't entirely explain the Arigna miner's experience.

As a pitman you definitely took pride in your skills, but you couldn't say at heart it was love of the job that had you working in the coalmines; you did it for the money. So whenever industrial unrest brought work to a halt, in many respects we weren't necessarily angry with our employers, we were wrestling with the very nature of what it meant to work underground for a living. The frustration and resentment we felt were directed against ourselves and our lot in life. Because wages alone could never make up for the harshness of the job; there had to be respect for the skills passed from generation to generation of coalminers, and respect too for the humiliations and privations suffered daily such a cruel distance beyond the reach of God's daylight. Our struggles might have looked to an outsider like they were about pay and conditions, but inwardly it was an argument with fate. On the surface we might have fought with our employers, but deep down we were battling our destiny.

# FOOTPRINTS

WE MOURN IN PUBLIC but we grieve in private. And facing into another winter we kept having the same thought: that if our friend Ronan had only stuck around he would have enjoyed this cosy gathering, this lovely meal, this closing of the day amongst friends.

But he had ended his life..

And being gone forever made him intensely present to us: he was the one person in our world who was always not there.

Then in the run-up to Christmas the weather forecasters began to predict heavy snowfalls. Yet with the days still dry and clear as the Artic front approached, Cathy and I decided to pack a rucksack and get out of the house.

For some reason we felt drawn to the mountains, and so driving around by the lake we turned off near the boathouse and took the byroad that rises through a mature planting of commercial Sitka spruce. We gained height quickly. Then at the fourth bend in the forest road we parked in a gravelled lay-by. Almost opposite the lay-by a footpath opened through the pines.

The air within the conifer plantation was calm, silent and scented with resin and damp earth. The fallen pine needles had melded into a peat-brown underlay on the forest floor that dampened and absorbed our footfalls Apart from the predominant vertical of the pines this was a dim and lifeless domain and even the regimented tree trunks had the look of an overrun palisade after a lost battle.

Coming out of the gloomy pinewood we traversed a deep gorge, following the path under a wooded slope on one side, while on the other side a sheer limestone cliff stood crowned in concentrated blue sky: a cliff face so imposing it generated a corona of pure silence.

We could be in Nepal or taking a high Alpine pass, and underfoot a light dusting of snow lay on the ground, making the bare hard clay of the path a rich umber. The shadows too were deep and strong against the clear December sunlight bouncing off the south facing cliff wall.

Sheep with spray painted markings ran on ahead of us as we started up the lower slopes. Our ribcages heaved for breath, unaccustomed to the exercise and the chill open air after being shut up so long in our house of grief.

We stopped and passed around the water bottle. Here and there stood weathered and wind-combed hawthorns with a filigree of sheep's wool caught in the thorns. Underfoot was a gully of loose stones dislodged by the streams of water that had sluiced down these hills throughout months of rain.

The climb took us up the side of the mountain close to a waterfall. Stopping more often now to catch our breaths we turned to face a calendar shot image of pine forest, sunny slopes and crystalline white snow in pockets in the valley. We were high enough now to see the bright reaches of the lake again on which we hadn't gone boating since Ronan died.

It struck me that until I looked at the lake I hadn't thought about Ronan. And even now his memory quickly gave way to the more sunny thought that in the day-to-day conduct of our lives we forget how much life enriching beauty there is in the world. We'd spent months cooped up at home, and here, fifteen minutes away by car and as many more minutes hiking up this slope, we had this magnificent situation. The world insists on being beautiful if we have a mind to see it

Puffing hard uphill and making several more stops for a dizzy appreciation of the height we'd gained, the path began at last to level out. And just before the upper plateau we stopped by a stony bottomed stream running and rippling over rocks.

A roofless hut stood next to the stream, a shelter for a cowherd grazing stock on these heights in the summer months. It made a lovely place to rest, open our flask of coffee and share around the food we'd packed in a hurry: cheese and bread and fruit that tasted like we were feasting on the very marrow of life.

"Life is good," I said to Cathy.

"I love you," she said.

We allowed ourselves a moment of unforced contentment. Though as the air grew colder and our limbs began to stiffen we stood up and set out again.

The walk took us eastwards along the edge of the cliff: the sort of cliff from which you try to keep a safe distance back but can't help taking a peek over the edge just to feel the tension grip your stomach at the inhuman remorselessness of the drop.

Looking south the sky was sparkling blue and the sun shining. But at our backs the dark clouds were piling in from the artic North. Mighty black juggernaut clouds freighted with snow, snow that would fall fast and heavy this high up, smudging and erasing our navigational landmarks and blotting out the trail.

On the next mountain the transmitter mast was already lost from view in a driving blizzard. I hurried the pace. But while I didn't want to alarm Cathy, I was no longer certain we were on the right path. What had been the clear impression of a sheep-path in the heather only minutes before was now whitening under deceptively random flakes knitting quickly into a featureless covering of snow.

We were ill prepared for a blizzard of this intensity. Yet rather than risk going astray or stumbling blindly into a bog hole, or over the edge of that fearsome drop, in the dwindling visibility and this increasingly treacherously blank snowfield, we would soon be forced to stop until the storm blew over. Already the light had dimmed to a sulphurous yellow and this false twilight would quickly give way to actual nightfall.

And then I saw it. In the fresh snow on the ground I noticed the unsullied imprint of a walker's boot. Somebody had just passed this way. It seemed strange that we had spotted no one, but in a wilderness innocent of other creatures it lifted our hearts to come on this trace of another human being. We were not alone on the mountain. Some guiding soul had passed our way, the direction of the footprints pointing our path home.

We pressed on with conviction, following the footprints that led over the next rise beyond which we could see a low spot in the fence around a commercial pine forest serviced by the road that gave us our way down off the mountain. And it was at this point exactly the footprints vanished.

Possibly the snow was coming down so thickly the boot-prints had been covered over. But they did not simply peter out; they came to an abrupt stop.

"That's odd," I said, without adding how strange it was that, despite the freshness of the tracks in the snow, we never once caught sight of our phantom hill-walker.

What came into my mind were those accounts of high altitude climbers who, in moments of extremity, have had an eerily convincing sense of the presence of another climber in the vicinity- an unseen but benevolent presence keeping them company, stewarding them out of their predicament: a role I could imagine our dead friend fulfilling out of love beyond the grave.

Whatever the truth might be, it made a heart-lifting change to think of him in this new light: not as the spectre of sorrow and loss that had shadowed our lives since his death, but as a mysterious agent of deliverance: a guardian presence determined to see that we came to no harm.

With the weather worsening, I had time only to offer up a mental 'thank you' as we squeezed through a hole in the fence around the plantation and began the straightforward hike back to the main road.

As we trooped downhill the snowflakes started coming down with greater insistence. And with this ghostly benediction dropping on our heads we stopped to share a sense of sudden wild rapture.

I felt a surge of the purest wonder running up and down my spine at the immensity of what was happening before us: the unfathomable swirling of elements that at one and the same time could be life threatening and life enriching. The ceaseless interplay of the negative and the positive like the falling flakes that appeared dark against the sky but changed to white as they reached the ground. With our faces raised to the heavens we received each delightful downward drifting snowflake, feeling the brush of each uniquely compounded fleck on our eyelashes and hot cheeks, soft and lovely and melting into our bodies like love itself; knowing that no matter what threatens or enriches the course of our daily lives, the happiness of loving is the only happiness there is.

# THE SUN ROOM

MY MOTHER SITS IN THE SUN ROOM. The twin glass doors look out on the lawn, beyond which the surrounding meadow field tapers into wetlands crisscrossed by drains that empty into the sea. After the reed-beds and bog, low hills rise, the fields divided into what the landowners call 'long squares' made of shorn meadows and open pastures. A band of farmhouses and agricultural buildings stands just shy of the wind-raked crest. My mother loves this view. She spends her days in her dressing gown watching the comings and goings of farm machinery and animals.

I had not expected her to make herself so at home in this treeless, sea-light saturated space. And it's true that at a certain time each day she orders the curtains pulled against the sun, so she can watch the television. She has what she calls 'a catch' in her groin, and can no longer get about safely on her own. I help her to the couch, where she can lie down with a blanket over her legs. The passing intimacy of real-life documentaries on the television takes her mind off the sharp reality of her predicament. Just as the double glazed sun room moderates the force of the weather outdoors, the television insulates her from the hard actuality of what stands in front of her.

Most days, a grey statuesque bird I call a heron, but country people like my mother call 'a crane', visits the bog drain. We sit in the sun room watching. The heron by tradition is a bird of healing. But my mother has already been through the chemotherapy, and gone into remission for six months, only for the cancer to flare up again, aggressive and unstoppable.

Today, as we study the motionless heron, a brown hare hops into view. In a few quick bounds the hare crosses the lawn to go around by the gable of the house. As the hare passes we both look into its big, wild and yet so desperately human eyes.

"We were going to give the house a name – 'Harefield," I tell my mother. "Because we often spotted a brown hare in the field when the house was being built. Only the hare has mixed meanings, not all of them lucky."

"Harefield, for sure," she says, looking at the lost hair in her hand as the latest hank comes lose from her head. Then she tries to smile, and I support the effort with an uncomfortable chuckle. She chuckles along with me saying, "I suppose it's all you can do."

My nights are spent apart from my wife Cathy, on an airbed on the floor in the downstairs bedroom. I keep a torch by my pillow, ready to help my mother if she stirs in the night time. My sleep is broken, the nights passing in a state of suspense, hanging on the next call. Mostly I get a sense that she is stirring and I wake up without having to be called.

"Are you all right?" I whisper.

"I'm sorry," she says. And I get up, help her out of bed, and escort her to the toilet.

Three times last night, at 3am, at 6.15am and again before 7am. She's tired, dehydrated, deeply upset at the loss of her independence.

She rests late into the morning, and I get on with my own jobs, blessed that I can work from home. She can signal that she needs help using a wire-free doorbell we picked up in Mary's of Sligo. She presses the button on the locker in the bedroom and I hear the battery-powered ringer sound in the kitchen.

I bring her breakfast in bed, usually a small bowl of porridge and tea and a single slice of buttered brown bread with marmalade. She still asks me to go easy on the butter because she's watching her cholesterol.

"How are you this morning," I ask.

"I'm very disappointed," she says. "I have no energy."

But then she gathers her strength and rises, saying, "We'll see what God has left out for me today."

The wig never comes off now. But when I suggest she might like to remove it, especially if it's making her head feel hot and her scalp prickly and it's just the two of us around the house all day, she says, "No". She is determined to keep the wig on at all times, because she doesn't want to end up like her neighbour John McManus. Even though he got new dentures she kept meeting him without his teeth. 'I'm leaving them out,' he told her, 'Until I get used to them'.

When she is not in the sun room looking at the farmers going about their business or watching the wildlife – the hare, the heron and lately a fine cock pheasant – she rests on the couch in the sitting room and tops up her addiction to daytime television. Not the 'nuts and sluts' of the American TV talk shows. She has the starting times memorised of the programmes on gardening, antiques, and cookery: *Secret Gardens*, *Flog It*, and *Ready Steady Cook*.

I'm glad of the time she spends watching the television, leaving me free to get on with my jobs, but there are times when I wish she would turn off the television and talk about what's happening.

The other night I heard her cry out, 'God help me make a decision'.

The new round of chemotherapy sessions is going harder on her than the illness itself, and there is the prospect that if the first couple of sessions don't yield results the treatment will be stopped.

Only obliquely, however, throughout months of treatment, remission and then the return of the cancer, have I heard her mention death.

At the start, she'd been admitted to the hospital with internal bleeding that we hoped was caused by an ulcer. The tests eventually revealed what the doctors called 'a mass' in her stomach, and she was diagnosed as having non-Hodgkins Lymphoma.

She quickly developed jaundice, and then bumps appeared under the skin on her forehead at the hairline and the sides of her head.

She asked the Consultant if he could do anything to get rid of the awful colour. "I don't want to be laid out looking yellow," she told him.

She underwent a keyhole surgical procedure. The jaundice cleared. But the consultant ruled out further surgery.

"I'm glad," she said, "I was dreading the thought of surgery."

"But you do know they want you to have chemo," I said.

The mention of chemo came as a shock. "When I heard I wouldn't be going under the knife," she said, "I didn't listen to the rest."

She met the oncology team again.

Out of earshot of my mother, they let me know she might live for six weeks without having chemotherapy, and then there would be a rapid onset of terminal symptoms.

She consented to undergo six sessions of chemo and opted for the strongest available treatment for a woman her age.

After taking the elevator up to the Day Oncology Unit, the nurse specialist welcomed my mother, and then weighed her ahead of the first session. "Are you ready?" the nurse asked, leading my mother along the 5th floor corridor.

My mother said, "I'd sooner be facing a bungee jump out that window."

Along with the chemo she was given a lot of tablets to take; steroids that made her giddy, tablets for her stomach, tablets to protect her kidneys and tablets to prevent water retention to reduce the swelling in her ankles. They kept her in overnight to monitor how she was responding. "18 times I went to the toilet," she told me when I visited her the next day. "I wasn't allowed go on my own, so every time I had to ring the nurse to get help. The whole night it was jingle bells all the way."

"She's a concert," the nurse said.

She was also a true farmer: one of those hardy women you see with a headscarf tied under the chin out running small farms of land by their own resources. Nobody I knew understood cattle better, she had a knowledge and a sympathy for animal ways and moods and the natural world unique to earlier generations. And she had too what locally would be called the 'concait' of the McDaid's: a proud woman who always found satisfaction in the fine condition of her livestock, and that the milk she and her husband in his day sent in churns to the creamery passed the hygiene and quality tests for the bonus added to that all important Kiltoghert creamery cheque.

And when during the chemo she took an unquenchable craving for cold fresh milk, she told the staff on the ward bringing her one glass after another that she'd 'need a cow tied at the door'.

She coaxed a smile too from her Consultant and his team when she said that after the chemo session there was enough fur on her tongue 'to make a hat'.

The nurses and specialists doted on her. And she found a

likeminded buddy in the porter in Day Oncology when the harsh spell of weather prompted him to tell her about his neighbour who still had a shed full of baled hay at the end of the winter because if he needed fodder again to see him through a late cold snap, 'he'd sooner be looking at it than looking for it.'

After two sessions of chemo the Consultant said he was pleased with her progress. The stent in her liver had cured the jaundice. The chemo had started to shrink the lymphoma and the bumps on her head had gone down.

She thanked him for her beauty treatment.

"What do you mean?" he asked.

"You took the green look off me and got rid of me horns."

As it turned out, helping my mother through the chemo was like minding a new baby, keeping her warm, fed and secure, giving her regular measured feeds, limiting visitors and looking out for tell tale signs of a temperature and early warnings of an infection. Above all, she had to be kept warm, prompting her to say about the tropical temperature inside our house, "Having me around is like keeping a snake."

Every three weeks she underwent chemo. She got on well, but found the hair loss distressing. She'd always taken trouble over her hair. Never spending large amounts of money at the hairdressers, but working on it herself in front of the bathroom mirror at home, putting in rollers ever night, and when the rollers came out, she used countless cans of hairspray regardless of the wear and tear on the ozone layer.

The family took turns minding her: sometimes she stayed with me and Cathy, and at other times she stayed in my brother and his wife's house. After driving her to the hospital at the start of another session I got on the phone to my brother to make arrangements with him at what time to collect her at the end of the session to take her to his home. When the call ended my mother told me about Michael Tymon. A woman from home hired him to drive her to the hospital. She didn't know how long she would be kept in. But she was anxious to have some arrangement in place to take her home again. Michael worked as a hackney driver, but he was also the local undertaker, prompting him to tell the poor woman, "Don't worry, Mam. One way or another, I'll be back to collect you."

We made light of these visits to the Day Oncology Unit and what might or might not be the outcome. But even in my full health the place gave me the heebie-jeebies, seeing so many people, from school goers to pensioners hooked to chemical tubing. The barrels of those big syringes carrying mixtures so corrosive that the individuals who made them up in advance needed to wear goggles and heavy duty gloves to protect themselves from the corrosive effects of the chemicals used to scald these manifold cancers into submission.

The three week cycle also meant that my mother kept meeting the same people. And taking her place in a plush reclining chair she was often seated next to the same man, a retired school bus driver called Andy. He told my mother this was his third time to go through with the chemo. And in between sessions he was on the full of a small bucket of tablets, he said, the half of which he threw out.

"You kept the weight on," my mother said on another visit towards the end of the full course of treatment.

"I do eat six times a day whether I'm hungry or not," Andy said.

"A nurse from America told me that."

"And you kept your hair."

"I did."

"Mine's gone," my mother said.

"I've seen a hairy donkey and a bald donkey on the bog," Andy told her. "And they were both doing the same work."

"I always asked God to take me with a heart attack," she told me at the end of that first round of chemo therapy sessions. "And when I heard about the cancer I felt that God deserted me."

"You could still go on to die of that heart attack," I said.

But in a roundabout way she had been letting me know that the day she learned she had cancer was the day her feeling of life long immunity from the worst possible news ended. And when she was called back several weeks later, and the multidisciplinary team said that the chemo had worked, and they gave her the 'all clear', she had trouble adjusting to the news. She couldn't accept the idea of remission.

Her complaints of stomach cramps, diarrhoea, constipation, tingling limbs, and numb fingers continued; until I was on the brink of asking her: "How well do you want to be?"

She went back to her own home and took to gardening again,

tending to her tomato plants in the greenhouse and the rose beds and her potted Ginkgo tree, a species she said, that had proved immune to the effects of the radiation from the bombs dropped on Hiroshima.

She got from July to December; then immediately after Christmas, the symptoms of the earlier lymphoma returned and she ended up back in the hospital.

She opted once more for chemo treatment, with the warning that unless immediate results were evident it would be useless to continue. Asked about side effects this time round she said, "I have a heartburn you could boil a kettle on."

"Anything else?"

"I feel like someone threw me in a bed of nettles," she said. "I have a scalding and a tingling all over and I can't feel the tips of my fingers."

She could be very precise when it came to describing her symptoms. And as the tingling grew more severe she equated this second lot of chemo with the rapid loss of mobility as the catch in her groin became near total loss of power in her legs. Then, unknown to any of her family, the Consultant and his team met with her during another short period of hospitalisation. He told her the chemo hadn't worked.

I got a frantically agitated call from her hospital bed. By the time I got to the hospital, however, she was somewhat calmer. She said one of the younger doctors sat with her a long time and answered her questions. She didn't say what the questions were. She said she was very upset, but when the young doctor left she found something on the television.

The Palliative Care team stepped in. They were not long by her bedside before my mother began to cry, not tears, just damp eyes and a fallen face, her chin down on her chest. Then from the bottom of her soul there rose a low howling wail of loss. But just as quickly she recovered, and she said she'd love to shove her hands in the clay, and to be gardening again. Only she knew she'd never see her snowdrops or her hellebores again. Or find out if her camellias had budded after the frost.

"You could take pictures, maybe," one of the care team suggested.

"Set yourself little goals," the other carer said, "and when you meet them set new ones.'"

But it was not small goals my mother wanted to set, she wanted to live. And she asked again for the doctors to come up with some further treatment. More chemo if needed. It fell to me to make it clear to her that the doctors had done their best, but there were no further treatments available. Trying to find a way to express it I said, "They're out of magic bullets."

These days, the Palliative Care people make me think of midwives at the other end of life, here to help us not into but out of this world. And with the home supports we've been given my mother is installed in a hospital bed in the downstairs bedroom where there is also enough room for an airbed for me.

"I'd give Ireland over if I could walk properly," my mother says. But this swelling of the ankles, I've seen before. You can almost tell how long a person has left to live by the rate of increase in the swelling of the ankles. "If I live to get over this," she says and begins her tablet taking routine, meticulously following the thrice daily ordered compartments of the blister packs, recovery bent, and determined not to die.

My friend Leland Bardwell calls to see my mother, but also to see me and how I am coping.

"When you were growing up, were you the one that was asked to do the messages?" Leland asks.

"I was," I tell her.

"You see – you were always reliable."

The challenge for me now is to moderate the force of my concern for my mother, the way the sunroom moderates the raw weather outdoors. I have to let her be and let her go. All the same, I'm never happier than when she can eat something tasty I've prepared. And as her appetite fails my hopes plummet and my anguish increases.

Perhaps like the larger sized tablets that I have to grind to powder for her to mix with food to help them go down, she is taking in the inevitability of her death in manageable portions. At any rate, her inner life is hidden from me, though I cannot say precisely what it is I'm waiting for her to reveal, what secret, or what summation, or what mystery might be laid bare. Or why, when a person is dying, should there be this expectation that they should be wiser at the end than at any other time in life.

The attending GP visits and I tell her that my mother is not resigned. She can of course be as private, obstinate and determined as she chooses, but at the same time I'd like my mother to die in a peaceful frame of mind. And I think it would be better if she came to terms with what is happening, because the refusal to admit she is dying is not just a refusal of sympathy but of intimacy too.

"Have you thought about keeping a diary," the doctor asks my mother.

"I could keep one," she says. "But it would be too depressing. It would want to come with a valium. I'd have the whole country on valium reading it."

"Why do you say that?"

"Because I think I'm dying."

"And are you ready to die?"

"Not yet."

The wind roars outside, sucking flames up the chimney of the open fire in the sitting room where my mother sits having a talk with the doctor.

"There's a great draw on that fire," my mother changes the subject..

She has said all she wants to, and I comply by saying, "When we were working on the chimney the builder told us, 'if it doesn't draw smoke it'll draw tears'."

Full-time caring puts a stress on coupledom, especially when it comes to having time together. And just to be able to go for a walk by ourselves is a struggle. But the way Cathy has joined me in caring for my mother makes me realise what a lucky marriage I have made. And it is while Cathy is helping my mother get showered and ready for the day that my mother opens up enough to share her true feelings when she tells Cathy, "I could cry. I could cry my eyes out. But if I start crying now I'm never going to stop. So I'm not going to."

"And what did you say to her," I ask Cathy.

"What could I say? It would break your heart. So I said, 'Don't write yourself off yet'."

And with only days left to live my mother goes against the grain of her worsening condition to make one last trip. We organise for her to visit her own house to see her flower garden. She feels weak and sick when she wakes up. But this is her one and only chance and she knows it. She gets dressed and fixes her wig. We drive to her mountain farm home in Arigna, where my brothers are waiting to help her from the car into her wheelchair which we then manhandle down the steps before her front door. The house is clean and tidy with coal fires burning in the black Stanley Rayburn in the kitchen and the open fireplace in the sitting room. Her niece Susan has arrived from America, and though Susan maintains she is in Ireland to visit relations in the North, she has of course packed a black dress.

I push the wheelchair along the gravelled garden path, and my mother reaches out and touches the delicate petals of her flowering azalea that she has lavished so much care on; she sees her hellebores thriving and she pauses over the crocus, early daffodils and pheasant-eye narcissi; putting her fingers into the clay of pot plants, in the full knowledge that she will never see her garden or her greenhouse again.

"God bless you, that's great," she says enjoying a cup of tea afterwards. Then, intuitively restoring her position as head of the household, she sits in her armchair beside the kitchen fire, and she asks Susan if she remembers her late father's favourite yarn about the boxer who made the sign of the cross, blessing himself as he stepped into the ring; and when the water-and sponge boy asked the trainer, 'Will that help', the trainer said, 'not if he can't box'.

The deadlines we set are ignored for as long as my mother's stories and her strength hold up, and the pain holds off. But then we really have to go.

I do the driving, taking us back up the lane where spring primroses flower on the banks in fragrant creamy clumps, and the hillside overlooking the farmhouse is newly green with a fresh growth of bracken, Our Lady's fern, or '*raithneach*' as we call it.

As we were leaving the house, Susan had said to me, 'The hill will be empty without her'.

And now, in my mind's eye, I see my mother years before, on the side of this same hill, cutting the new growth of *raithneach* with a scythe; working with that antique implement in full view of her neighbours as an example and a rebuke.

The farm has several of these hillside fields that are too steep to safely work with a tractor. But each summer she stubbornly mapped out a square of raithneach for herself to cut by hand each day while my brothers and I refused to relieve or join her. We couldn't see the point. No matter how often you cut it there was no getting this rampant and invasive bracken under control without machinery. And in a situation where you know you are beaten before you begin, I had come to look on her obstinate determination as pride making a spectacle of itself; only to understand now as I close the road gate a final time that what drives determination is the mystery of how much we care.

By the end of the following day her bed-rest has deepened into a coma from which she cannot wake. For two more days we are attentive but helpless, listening to her laboured breathing, every few hours turning her body that is now as limp as a ragdoll. The moment nears. And with everyone present in the downstairs bedroom, the windows are showered with hailstones. A big gust of wind shakes the house, as if taking her soul with it, and then just as she goes, the heavens open.

# ACKNOWLEDGEMENTS

Many thanks to Danielle Kerins for handling the editing, formatting and publication of this book and to Niall Kerrigan for designing the beautiful cover, also credit to Cormac O'Leary for providing the artwork.

'The Last Mining Village', 'A Good One', 'Last Remains', 'Out With It', 'On The Market', 'Departures', 'A Small Rebellion', 'Cuckoo Visits' 'Cloudburst' (originally titled 'New Islands') first published unrevised in Departures by Brian Leyden, Brandon Book Publishers, Ireland, 1992. 'Christmas Promise' first published unrevised in Departures and Irish Christmas Stories II, ed. David Marcus, Bloomsbury, London, 1997. 'Florida Coast' is a revised version of the story first published in The Alphabet Garden – European Short Stories, ed Pete Ayrton, Brandon Book Publishers, Ireland, 1994. 'The Lake of Brightness' first published in The Clifden Anthology, ed Brendan Flynn, Ireland 2004. 'Footprints' in abridged form first published in This Landscape's' Fierce Embrace (the poetry of Francis Harvey) ed Donna L. Potts, Cambridge Scholars Publishing, UK, 2013. 'The Sun Room' in highly abridged form first published as 'Death of a Countrywoman' in Sunday Miscellany (a selection from 2008 – 2011) ed. Clíodhna Ní Anluain, New Island, Ireland, 2011. 'Christmas Lights' broadcast on Sunday Miscellany Live at Christmas, National Concert Hall, Dublin, 2013.

73565221R00092

Made in the USA
Columbia, SC
17 July 2017